SHANGHAI STEAM

edited by
Ace Jordyn, Calvin D. Jim, and Renée Bennett

Absolute XPress
AN IMPRINT OF HADES PUBLICATIONS, INC.
CALGARY

Shanghai Steam
Copyright © 2012
All individual contributions copyright
by their respective authors.

This is a work of fiction. Names, characters, places, and
incidents are the products of the author's imagination or
are used fictitiously and are not to be construed as real.
Any resemblance to actual events, locales, organizations, or
persons, living or dead, is entirely coincidental.

Absolute XPress
An Imprint of Hades Publications Inc.
P.O. Box 1714, Calgary, Alberta, T2P 2L7, Canada

Edited by Ace Jordyn, Calvin D. Jim, and Renée Bennett
Interior design by Janice Blaine
Cover Illustration by James Ng
ISBN: 978-1-77053-022-5

Absolute XPress and Hades Publications, Inc. acknowledges the ongoing support
of the Alberta Foundation for the Arts and the Canada Council for the Arts for
our publishing programme.

Library and Archives Canada Cataloguing in Publication

Shangai steam / edited by Ace Jordyn, Calvin D. Jim,
and Renee Bennett.

ISBN: 978-1-77053-022-5
(e-Book ISBN: 978-1-77053-023-2)

1. Science fiction, Canadian (English). 2. Short stories,
Canadian (English). 3. Canadian fiction (English)--21st
century. I. Jordyn, Ace II. Jim, Calvin D III. Bennett,
Renee

PS8323.S3S53 2013   C813'.087620806   C2012-906616-8

FIRST EDITION
(D-20121016)
www.absolute-x-press.com

Table of Contents

Acknowledgements
Ace Jordyn, Calvin D. Jim, and Renée Bennett

Introduction: When Worlds Collide.....................................1
Jay Lake

The Fivefold Proverbs of Zhen Xiaquan...........................3
Tim Ford

Qin Yun's Mechanical Dragon and the Cricket Spies........9
Amanda Clark

Moon-Flame Woman...17
Laurel Anne Hill

Love and Rockets at the Siege of Peking..........................26
K. H. Vaughan

The Master and the Guest...37
Crystal Koo

Ming Jie and the Coffee Maker of Doom.........................45
Brent Nichols

A Hero Faces the Celestial Empire;
A Death by Fire is Avenged by Water...............................50
Julia A. Rosenthal

Riding the Wind..60
William H. Keith

Mistress of the Pearl Dragon..70
Shen Braun

Song of My Heart...77
Jennifer Rahn

Last Flight of the Lóng Qíshì..85
Emily Mah

Protection from Assassins..90
Frances Pauli

Seeds of the Lotus...97
Camille Alexa

The Ability of Lightness..109
Tim Reynolds

Fire in the Sky...115
Ray Dean

The Legend of Wong Heng Li.....................................121
Frank Larnerd

Flying Devils...127
Derwin Mak

Legend of the Secret Masterpiece.............................138
Nick Tramdack

Jing Ke Before the Principle of Order........................151
Minsoo Kang

·•✻•·

Acknowledgements

Our deepest gratitude goes to Brian Hades at EDGE Science Fiction and Fantasy Publishing for boldly steaming ahead into the world of wuxia.

Thank you to those who contributed to the editors' vision including Anna-Marie Bortollotto for her help with the anthology and unceasing enthusiasm; Tereasa Maille for her knowledge of Chinese language, history and culture; Celeste Peters of *Elegant Edge Website Design* for the website design; Jay Lake for a great introduction; James Ng for the incredible Chinese steampunk art that graces our cover and Janice Blaine for taking that art and creating a breathtaking cover.

Special thanks to family and friends for their encouragement including Jennifer, Yoshi and Tosh for giving Calvin the time to live in a martial arts-steampunk fantasy world and patiently waiting for him to return to earth; and to Doug Cooney for his support.

And finally, thanks to fellow writers at IFWA (Imaginative Fiction Writers' Association) who are an inspiration to writers everywhere.

When Worlds Collide

Jay Lake

Talking about writing is always an act of approximation. Perhaps not so extreme as dancing about architecture, as the tools of both fiction and critique are still words, often uttered by the same people in the same conversations. Still, we grope our way toward understanding with the same tools that we use to grope our way toward satori through fiction.

All that being said, one of the things writers say about writing is that a story is an intersection of two ideas. Conflicting agendas. Characters in adversity. Worlds colliding. Cat and mouse.

Wuxia and steampunk.

Shanghai Steam is precisely that intersection. The classic Chinese tradition of *wuxia* draws from hundreds of years of morality tales and political epics grounded in martial arts and the role of the individual-as-hero. Steampunk has been all the rage this past decade and more, drawing on pseudo-Victorian technology and culture to interrogate our own contemporary social evolution, permanently stuck as it seems to be on fast forward. Together, they fight crime!

Well, okay, not fighting crime. But together, the two forms seem capable of taking on almost any other task. The stories in *Shanghai Steam* have settings ranging from Mars to ancient China. They move from microcosmic journeys of individual courage to epic (if pocket-sized) landscapes of mechanical autonomy and cultural clash. Like any good volume of stories, these snag at the mind like nets cast into the stream of imagination.

Likewise, *Shanghai Steam* brings established writers such as *New York Times* bestseller William H. Keith and the incisively brilliant Camille Alexa together with new story-tellers just emerging, such as Amanda Clark and K. H. Vaughn. A range of talents, viewpoints, and cultures is represented here.

One of the particular joys of this book for me was reading the capsule biographies of the authors. There are a number of writers in *Shanghai Steam* of Asian ancestry, some resident now in Asia, others living in the United States and Canada. Given the perpetual tension in the speculative fiction field between the imperative to write the Other and the need to provide balanced, nuanced views of multiple cultures, it's gratifying to see editors Ace Jordyn, Calvin D. Jim and Renée Bennett stepping forthrightly up to provide a table of contents that acknowledges cultural authority and life experience.

Action? Adventure? Bare knuckle brawling? Exotic technology? China — ancient, modern and future? It's all here in *Shanghai Steam*.

I hope you enjoy this book as much as I did.

Jay Lake

Portland, OR
August, 2012

The Fivefold Proverbs of Zhen Xiaquan

Tim Ford

Li Sen sat beside his master, the great poet and philosopher, Zhen Xiaquan, watching him die. For his entire life of eight and twenty years, Li Sen had faithfully followed every command, saw to every need, and fulfilled every promise. Yet now, in this, his final vigil, he saw no way to succeed.

"My words must not die," whispered Zhen Xiaquan from cracked, dry lips. "Do not let me be lost to memory."

Li Sen reassured him, "Your words are recorded on the scrolls of the Imperial Archive, great thinker. They are preserved in the memories of all China."

Zhen shook his head. "Paper is weak. It frays apart, burns, turns to dust. Just as my body will turn to dust. I have seen the future, my loyal servant. The future is in iron."

"Iron?"

"Yes." Zhen coughed harshly, spitting a glob of blood onto his chin. "There is a village on the outskirts of Canton, where an artisan of great skill, Cao Fan, resides. She is the only one who can help us."

"What shall I do, Master?"

"Find Cao Fan. Have her build an automaton to record my words. Build it in my image, to carry on my legacy."

Li Sen bowed and left his master's side. He had no idea what an automaton was or how it recorded words. He didn't know what village Cao Fan lived in or even what she looked like. Despite all this, Li Sen would not let his master down.

Li Sen took a large sack of coin, Zhen Xiaquan's portrait and his best walking stick, and set out for Canton down the Emperor's Road. He passed through a dark forest, where insects bit him and rain soaked him to the bone. From the deep shadows of the trees, animals howled and snarled at him. "All this hardship and more I endure for my master," Li Sen proclaimed. "I will make the journey, no matter the cost!"

The gods look kindly on loyalty, but less kindly on arrogance, and so Li Sen's words were quick to bring down their judgement. Three bandits sprang from the woods.

"Hold!" cried the leader. "You are travelling through our lands. As such, you must pay us a toll."

"This is the Emperor's road," Li Sen said.

The bandit leader wagged a finger at him. "No, I'm quite certain this belongs to me. I have lived here my whole life. Be a good boy and give us what is rightly ours."

Li Sen stepped back, prepared to turn and run. Instead, he slipped in the mud, scattering his master's coins. The bandits scrambled after the coins and Li Sen fled.

Now penniless, the faithful servant carried on with his mission. It took him two days to reach the outskirts of Canton, and another to discover where the famed artisan, Cao Fan lived. He found her house as it had been described: a simple one-story wooden home, with a yard filled with bits of metal, clockwork, and other machine scraps strewn about.

Li Sen picked his way through the yard, taking care not to disturb anything. He had been warned that Cao Fan was a woman of short temper who preferred to be left alone. Li Sen puffed up his chest to look important when he knocked on her door.

The woman who answered was much smaller and older than he had expected. Li Sen bowed and said, "I seek the great artisan, Cao Fan, on behalf of my master, Zhen Xiaquan."

The woman crossed her arms. "You have found her," she said.

Li Sen explained his mission. "But I have no money," he said. "Bandits stole it from me."

"Then why should I work for you?" she asked.

Li Sen fell to his hands and knees. "I ask for my master. He lies dying, and we must save his great words for the people."

"I do not know your master or his words. What meaning do words have to an artisan such as myself? No money, no automaton."

Li Sen would not see it end like this. "I will work for you then."

Cao Fan was genuinely surprised. "Work?"

"Whatever you require. I know how to clean. I can cook … a little. Until you feel you have been paid sufficiently."

Cao Fan considered this to be reasonable. For many days, Cao Fan set Li Sen to various tasks: bringing buckets of water from a nearby stream, organizing the scrap metal she had strewn about her home, cooking her meals, cleaning her floors, mending her roof … on and on and on.

One day Cao Fan took him into the woods. After a short walk, they came to a clearing in the woods where a massive boulder sat, collecting moss but otherwise doing very little.

"I want you to move that rock," Cao Fan said.

Li Sen's jaw dropped.

"I need it for the raw ore. Of course, if you no longer want the automaton…"

Li Sen scowled. His hands were raw from scrubbing floors, his back ached, his sandals were crumbling apart and he knew he could not move the boulder. But, loyalty to Zhen Xiaquan and his own sense of honour demanded that he try. With a grunt, Li Sen set himself against the boulder. He groaned and heaved, strained and pulled, pushed and begged the heavens to give him more strength.

Finally, Cao Fan said, "Stop."

Li Sen collapsed against the boulder.

Cao Fan smiled for the first time in all the days he had been with her. "I am impressed, little man," she said. "Your loyalty to your master is firm. Such loyalty deserves to be rewarded. I will create his automaton."

Li Sen grinned like a mad fool.

While Cao Fan built the automaton Li Sen gladly cooked her meals and cleaned her home. The finished iron figure looked just like Zhen Xiaquan. Its limbs moved just as Zhen Xiaquan did when he spoke to his people, arms spread wide as if embracing the whole world. Inside of it was a recording cylinder made of polished steel that would record Zhen Xiaquan's wisdom and then play it back.

"But only five proverbs," Cao Fan warned him.

"Only five?"

"Yes. If you record more then you risk losing them all. Now, you must go. Your master is waiting."

Li Sen bowed and left. He strapped the heavy automaton to his back, and in four days, walked back home. He immediately went to his master's side and told him what had happened. Zhen's eyes filled with tears of pride and gratitude.

"You have done well, my loyal friend," he said. "Now, my words will live on."

Li Sen looked ashamed. "But Master," he said, "you must know that only five proverbs can be recorded."

"It is all right," said the wise poet. "Five proverbs will grant me immortality. Please, help me choose."

So, late into the night, the great philosopher dictated all of his proverbs. Li Sen basked in Zhen Xiaquan's infinite wisdom and his soul was uplifted by the glowing prose. Bit by bit, they whittled that body of work down to five pieces:

1) A cherry blossom late in bloom may hold the greatest beauty.
2) The cornered rat knows when to play dead.
3) The mightiest army is only as strong as its weakest soldier.
4) All jade begins raw; only through polishing does its true worth shine through.
5) The sun rises and sets on young and old alike.

Li Sen recorded the five proverbs as Cao Fan had instructed.

When the final character was dictated, he played back the recording. The automaton whirred and waved its arms and recited the proverbs perfectly. Nevertheless, Li Sen was unhappy. The journey for this machine had been so difficult. He had been robbed, deceived, and abused. Surely, Li Sen reasoned, it couldn't hurt to add just one more proverb?

Praying to the gods for forgiveness, Li Sen dictated one more proverb, then played back the recording. The result was flawless. Li Sen was overjoyed. Then he considered the list in his hand once more. So, he recorded another. And another. Li Sen admitted that he might be pushing his luck. On the other hand, nine was a very lucky number … so he recorded one more. The machine recited the proverbs flawlessly, and Li Sen grinned, at last pleased.

Zhen Xiaquan smiled sagely at his servant. "Thank you, Li Sen," Zhen said. "I go now to join my ancestors, knowing that my legacy lives on." And so the Great Philosopher Zhen Xiaquan died with dignity and grace.

The next day, Li Sen took the automaton into town for it to recite Zhen Xiaquan's nine proverbs. Without hesitation, the automaton said:

"A cherry blossom late in bloom may hold the greatest beauty. The cornered rat knows when to play dead. The mightiest army is only as strong as its weakest soldier. All jade begins raw; only through polishing does its true worth shine through. The sun rises and sets on young and old alike."

And then it fell silent. Only five of the nine proverbs had been recited. Li Sen waited, but Zhen Xiaquan's likeness remained silent and still. Li Sen sidled up to the machine and gave it a tiny kick.

"All cornered rats begin raw."

Li Sen's eyes widened. The crowd muttered in confusion. Li Sen reset the machine and played it again. This time, the automaton said:

"The polished sun late in bloom is the mightiest army.

"A cherry blossoms true worth shines on young and old alike.

"All jade knows its weakest beauty."

Li Sen silently cursed himself. Not only was it not playing all nine proverbs, it was now mixing up the five. Some of the crowd started to boo, others picked up rocks to throw, but then one voice called out: "New proverbs! New proverbs!"

Li Sen raised an eyebrow.

A skinny boy in the crowd excitedly jumped up and down. "Don't you see?" he said. "Zhen Xiaquan is in the machine. His spirit remains!"

The crowd dropped their rocks and cheered wildly. Li Sen smiled. Who was to say that there was no wisdom to be found in folly? Perhaps that was the true spirit of Zhen Xiaquan's philosophy.

"The mightiest army rises on the old rats," the automaton said.

"Well," Li Sen said. "Truer words were never said than 'what they don't know, can't harm them.' Let that be the proverb of my own life."

"Dead cherry blossoms hold the greatest raw beauty," confirmed the automaton.

So he left the machine to the people to spread his master's unique and wondrous wisdom. Years later, people everywhere remembered Zhen Xiaquan and his wonderful automaton, though no one recalled the name of Li Sen. Which suited that most loyal of servants just fine.

Tim Ford is a half-Chinese, half-Scottish author and playwright from Calgary. His plays have been staged by indie theatre companies *Mob Hit Productions* and *Sage Theatre*, and his short stories have appeared in several publications including *Crossed Genres* and *Neo-Opsis Magazine*. He currently resides in Toronto.

Qin Yun's Mechanical Dragon and the Cricket Spies

Amanda Clark

Qin Yun flattened herself against the wall of great grandfather's lab, as she still liked to call it. Her father had turned it into it a cricket hatchery. A waste. A complete waste. He hardly ever let her build anything.

Except for the little distiller for making *baijiu*. *That* he had use for.

A piercing screech cut the air as Qin Yun's mechanical dragon swooped past again, this time straight for the cricket cages, hovering over the one holding eight fat ones. Then it dove and latched on to the bamboo bars. It shoved its snout in between two of them and screeched frustration.

Worse than a steam engine with a damaged piston.

"Hush! You'll wake Father!"

The little dragon ignored her and forced its snout deeper between the staves.

Qin Yun dropped down and scrabbled over the stone tiles behind the massive marble-topped island in the center of the lab. It's first words had been a shock, coming, as they had, straight into her mind.

What do I eat?

It should have been obvious. A mechanical woken by *qi* would think itself flesh and blood, and be hungry. That would have been a good time to keep her thoughts to herself.

I don't know, maybe a fat juicy cricket…

She heard the pistons in the dragon's tiny steam engine chug faster, emitting fumes of burning *baijiu*. Then the dragon hissed.

Qin Yun popped her head up as the creature's filmy metallic wings whomped the air and dragged the cage off the shelf. The eight crickets, owed to a client the next day, chirped in terror.

"No!" she cried, springing up.

The dragon gave a mighty pull and flew out of reach. Then it flapped twice more before sinking toward the workbench.

Straight for the distiller.

One wingtip grazed the flame under the boiler and the thing screeched, banking. Dragon and cage plummeted downward.

Qin Yun dove to catch them but they crashed to the floor, then bounced down the sloping walkway out onto the newly laid marble courtyard. Usually only *laowai* in the French concession could afford marble courtyards but this was a gift from the Emperor, to show the status of their Shanghai *shikomen* estate. Qin Yun slipped and fell when her feet hit the marble.

The cage tumbled on, dragon still attached, toward the sandalwood gate. Qin Yun lurched up after the rolling cage.

The dragon and cage bumbled faster, finally slamming into the massive sandalwood gate. The cage latch sprang open and the cricket chirps shifted from fear to jubilation. Four of them sprang out, leaving four behind. Father would be furious if she didn't catch the escapees. Eight had been promised to an official in the Imperial household!

Then with clickity-clacking precision the dragon unwound its sinuous body from under the cage and pounced on the first of them. It gobbled down that one and the next, crushing the other two under foot. That left four still inside the cage, cheeping the code for "no, no, no!".

Qin Yun scooped up the little dragon, which sat up in her hands and snapped its toothy jaws as if pleased with itself. So life-like!

Qin Yun's pride swelled in spite of the mayhem she had caused. She *would* be a mechanic. And build lots more little dragons, to hunt down rebel death birds. They would never drop ordnance on the retinue guarding the crown prince again.

If only her White Lance service wasn't necessary.

"What is going on in here daughter?"

Qin Yun stiffened. Father still managed to sneak up on her, even though the din of mother's weapons practice had been gone from the house all these months.

Keeping her back to him as he came up, Qin Yun quickly flipped open the breastplate on the dragon's midsection, reached through cricket remains and twisted the small onyx crystal slaved to the steam engine. She wiped dead cricket goo on her pants.

With a last twitch the wings went still, then the bright red eyes dimmed to black. Qin Yun gasped as *qi* flowed back into her. She turned to her father, who glanced down at the dragon with disapproval.

"You will never pass your Ordeal if you play with toys more than you practice with your weapons," he warned. The hairs on Qin Yun's neck rose.

"What harm is there for me to study mechanicals? I have another year to get ready for the Ordeal."

Father's lips flattened into a line as he looked past her to the cricket cage with its four survivors. Qin Yun cringed as they sang in the Qin family code, "Hush! You'll wake Father!" repeating her words over and over.

Father brushed past her and crouched down to pick up the cage. His eyes went cold when he saw the two crushed crickets on the floor. He took several deep breaths, then stood up, latching the lid.

"Where are the other two?"

She moved the dragon behind her back. Father shook his head.

"What do you think Admiral Yehenara will say if I offer him *four* crickets when he comes tomorrow? He will say I mean his death!"

"These were for Yehenara?" Qin Yun couldn't hold back her shock. "How can the Emperor suspect his first wife's brother?"

Father's eyebrows rose slightly. "He is Manchu, of course." Mistrust of Manchu nobility was in the blood of Qin family, ever since the Manchu tried to usurp the first Ming emperor back in the 1400's.

Father shook his head, ignoring her question. He put his ear to the cage. "Four crickets ... or none. You've traumatized them."

Qin Yun moved closer, her face over the cage, and Father let her.

"Peace, little brothers," she sang softly, investing hope into the words. Emotions mattered when it came to crickets. She repeated the phrase, pausing after each time, waiting for the little spies to calm and clear their memories. She had practiced it in the homes of the high and mighty during her cricket tending visits, after harvesting coded conversations. An honorable job for those born to *wuxia* families.

Qin Yun cradled the dragon gently and stepped back.

"They will quiet soon."

"But still there are only four," Father said. He tucked the cage under one arm and held out his other hand. Qin Yun sighed then handed over her creation. He braced the mechanical beast against the cage and peered down in through the open breast plate. His thumb brushed the small cube of onyx.

"A *qi* crystal? This is very dangerous, daughter. Give it too much of your *qi* and you could lose yourself."

She hadn't expected him to recognize it. Attaching the onyx *qi* crystal to the engine was the key to making it so small. It eliminated the control drum. The entire engine was no bigger than a walnut.

Qin Yun stuck out her chin. "Better than the pierced metal rollers those horrible wind-up death birds use." His eyes went flat at the mention of death birds so she hurried on. "And I only breathed a little *qi* into it. To test the airworthiness, to see if it would—"

"Destroy half of our next shipment?"

Qin Yun curled her toes inside her cloth shoes and looked down at them, finding no proper response.

"Daughter, if I knew you would be sharing your *qi* with mechanicals—"

"But Father, you should have seen it fly!"

He didn't quite manage to suppress a smile. He handed back the dragon then rubbed the back of his neck.

"The only other cricket breeding concern in Shanghai is at the White Lance Chapter House." He took hold of her shoulder, his eyes stern. "You must take up White Lance early, to pay them for replacements. They won't take money for them."

The leaden look in his eyes as he brushed past chilled her. "I will request your invitation to the Ordeal."

Qin Yun's skin flashed fire and her heart hammered against her ribs. The Ordeal of the White Lance. She had always known she would face it. One member of every Qin generation submitted to it, ever since Qin Liangyu, the first Ming emperor's Honored Ally, led her White Lance troops against the Manchu usurper three hundred years ago. It was her family's sacred duty — her sacred duty.

"Now? I still have a year! Why not ask them to loan us four crickets, until we can replace them when the next clutch hatches!"

Father stopped, his eyes pitiless.

"Ever since Qin Liangyu saved the empire, this family has never begged a favor. Or failed to deliver what the Emperor needs. We will not start now."

"But … I'm not ready."

Her father twisted his lips as if he had just swallowed a rotten egg. "Then daughter, you will die."

The crickets fell silent.

Astride Ping, her mother's retired warhorse, Qin Yun trotted up *Liangmaqiao Lu*. Mother's white lance clicked against the sword sheathed at her hip. These weapons had followed mother into service for thirty years, the last five guarding the crown prince during his visits to Shanghai.

Until an assassin's death bird killed her.

Qin Yun couldn't even hate the prince for surviving the attack. She would never have been allowed to build mechanicals, had the Ming not come to power. Qin Yun sighed to settle her nerves, then kicked Ping forward into a trot.

The old gelding dropped back into a walk near the gate of White Lance Chapter House. Qin Yun dismounted and rang the heavy iron bell out front. The sun had gone down in the hours waiting for the invitation to come after Father sent word. The streets felt lonely. Only the clop-clop of a single-horse carriage broke the late night quiet. Inside a small lantern illuminated a young *laowai* woman and an older gentleman. A father and daughter, she thought, laughing together. Even as angry as she was at him, it made her miss Father.

Qin Yun handed Ping's reins to the apprentice who came to meet her. She gave him the scroll with the contract her father offered: her early entry to service in exchange for four cricket spies. She took the mechanical dragon from her saddle bag. When the stable man left, she opened the breast plate and looked into the dead black eyes of her clockwork beast.

"If I die, carry my last moments back to Father," she whispered. "So he knows I have honored our family." She breathed *qi* into it until the eyes glowed red.

Its fore claws flexed around her fingers and the jaws opened, emitting a lick of fire. The dragon spread wide its wings then hopped to her shoulder, digging into the thick cloth of her tunic. She pried the dragon loose and set it on the bell post, cautioning it to stay.

The door to the chapter house opened revealing a courtyard framed by dim walkways. Gaslights set along the second floor balcony rails cast flickering shadows on the flagstones.

Qin Yun brandished the white lance in one hand and held the sword down at her side, then stepped through to be greeted by the sound of steel scraping over leather. Mother's words rose up, given to her when she was barely old enough to hold a sword.

There is just the Ordeal. No ceremony. When you cross the threshold holding the White Lance they will come. You are a daughter of Qin Liangyu. Never forget who you are!

Five female warriors streamed into the courtyard, dressed head to toe in black. They drew swords as they formed a loose circle around her. The first one darted in, blade high, then swung down for an overhead cut.

Qin Yun's knees felt watery but she willed herself to stay upright as she met the blow. She twisted her sword so the adversary's blade slid harmlessly past her shoulder. Then a scrape of leather on stone to her left. She spun, extending her lance to sweep the opponent's feet. The others moved in, tightening the circle, so that any step back drove her into a different opponent. One cut split the fabric of her tunic, then there were two, then four, six, eight.

Eight shallow cuts. If any opponent judged her unfit, the cuts would turn lethal. She tried to return the blows, but her strikes were clumsy.

Cut, step back, cut, step back again.

The tallest of the warriors leveled a killing blow straight at Qin Yun's neck.

Qin Yun's mechanical dragon came screeching in and deflected the lethal blow.

Qin Yun looked on in horror as the dragon turned and dove at the warrior, tearing her hood to reveal a woman her mother's age. The warrior grabbed for the dragon but it darted away and looped for another run, this time flaming. Her tunic caught fire and the woman cursed. The dragon came around for a third attack.

"Stop!" yelled Qin Yun. She swung her blade to knock the dragon away. The warrior dropped to the ground, rolling while one of her friends followed, slapping at the fire. The others closed in on Qin Yun.

She raised her hands, and dropped her weapons, hoping surrender might save her, or at least salvage what was left of family honor. The dragon lay crumpled on the ground, and the sight of it broke her heart.

"Stand down!" shouted a man with a heavy German accent. His voice came from the shadows, at the end of the courtyard. Her opponents stepped aside and Qin Yun fell to her knees next to the broken dragon. The breastplate was bent in and she couldn't see if the engine was still intact.

A skinny *laowai* man with chopped yellow hair strode over, led by an ancient woman in a red *qipao*, her hair piled up on her head like a *Miao* matriarch. The *laowai* smelled of metal and smoke and his soot-stained shirt had tiny cinder burns all over it.

"Did you make that?" he asked, pointing at the dragon. She nodded, holding it loosely against her chest. The old woman laid a hand on his arm.

"Wait, Herr Dekker," she said, her eyes widening when they fell on the dragon. She turned to Qin Yun. "I am the Voice of this House. You will call me Older Sister." She gestured for Qin Yun to rise.

"A person so ill-prepared for the Ordeal, who chooses to protect a future sister by destroying a thing she loves … such a person shows promise."

Older Sister motioned to the shadows behind her. A girl ran up and handed her a metal medallion. A white lance blade had been etched in the center. She hung it around Qin Yun's neck.

"From now on," said Older Sister, giving her a scathing look, "your training, which is sorely lacking, is your first duty. The crickets will be delivered tonight. Welcome to White Lance Chapter House."

Qin Yun let out her breath and with it she felt her dream of becoming a mechanic drifting away.

But while she lived, there was hope. White Lance Troops led useful lives. They had purpose. She would hang on to that.

Giving up mechanicals was small penance to pay for her life. Wasn't it?

Older Sister glanced at the German in sooty clothes. "I believe our mechanic will have interest in this ingenious device."

Herr Dekker nodded and Older Sister turned back toward Qin Yun. "If you wish, you may become his apprentice during your free hours."

Qin Yun could barely breathe. All she ever craved was to hunch over a workbench, building things. Older Sister was not done.

"And I would not object, should he allow you to repair your dragon."

Qin Yun bowed to Older Sister. "If it pleases the Voice of the White Lance Chapter House."

Herr Dekker stepped closer and gave her a friendly wink. "Yah, and maybe we make a bigger one after that."

Older Sister clapped her hands and the courtyard was flooded by the women of the White Lance, coming to meet their newest sister.

Amanda Clark lives in Oregon and spent four years working in China. She has a PhD in Physics, two black belts, and is a graduate of Viable Paradise Writers Workshop. She hopes to read all the books and write all the stories she wants to before she dies.

Moon-Flame Woman

Laurel Anne Hill

The crumbling rock on the vertical face of the mountain yielded to Cho Ting-Lam's probing finger. It clung like crushed grains of rice to the crevice between her nail and skin. Her next target had a weak spot. Good.

The lowered, hanging basket holding her in the air swayed as she changed position and the late morning wind strengthened. Suspended ropes held by old Master Ye and his men far above her now snagged on jagged stone. Yet this Sierra Mountain was not her only adversary. Also formidable was that barbarian, Superintendent Brockton Tim. If only she knew Brockton's weak spot, she would target his corresponding lack of enlightenment.

Because of Brockton, she must break through five feet of this granite mountain before next twilight faded. Five feet. A distance equaling her height plus the length of her middle finger. Yesterday, when work on this new railway tunnel had begun, she — disguised as a man — and her fellow countrymen barely blasted through two feet. Failure today would further erode her dignity, although far less than when her father sold her into slavery. Failure could also explode her into countless fragments.

Once more, Ting-Lam leaned into the shallow excavation. This time she scratched with her long stick in the film of dirt on the rock face. She drew the Chinese characters representing her clan's hero, the brave swordsman Wu Sing. With luck, Wu Sing's harmony of spirit would ready this section of rock for her by stealing the stone's energy. If only he could erase her personal shame, too. Give her a husband and a chance to bear sons. Then she could cast off her male disguise, reveal the secret Master Ye already knew.

Oh, revered ancestor Wu, protector of the poor, she thought. *I need your power.* Beloved master of the martial arts, he was, resident of the bamboo spirit house that hung from the Gingko tree in her father's garden, so far away from California. She would need Wu's help, as always, when she again fired Master Ye's moon-flame gun at this wretched barrier of mountain stone. Well, her own *qi* and modest ability to affect its flow could not call forth the gun's mystical light and drill holes in granite. She was just a novice with weaponry, even less accomplished than she was at *Baguachang,* Master Ye's martial art.

"We have a tunnel to dig," old Master Ye called in Cantonese from his perch on a granite outcrop fifty feet up the mountainside. "Before 1868."

"Yes, Uncle." Such sarcasm. This was only 1866.

She always worked too slow or too fast. Bound her breasts too tight against her chest. Didn't bind them well enough. Ye, as critical as a new bride's mother-in-law, so often found fault with her actions. Still, Ye treated her far better than the other men who had owned her. And he understood this fledgling tunnel must grow five feet deeper by nightfall or Brockton would insist on using more dangerous explosive mixtures.

There. She completed the Chinese characters, the most important of the one hundred she could read and write. She stepped backward into the center of the basket, raised the goggles from her neck to her eyes, let her straw hat slip down against her upper spine, then hefted the weighty moon-flame gun to her shoulder. Keeping her balance in a rocking basket was no easy task. Sunlight glinted upon the round brass chamber and the slender barrel, flared at the base. The glass dial sparkled, ready. *All arises from emptiness. All returns to emptiness.* May the rock accept these sayings her grandmother had taught her.

Ting-Lam pressed the trigger.

A thin stream of blue light like mystical moon glow streamed from the gun's barrel and struck the target area, obliterating Ting-Lam's mark. Rock sizzled and spat. A little column of gray smoke arose, as though from an opium pipe. The smoke thickened, darkened and billowed. All things of this world interconnected. Ting-Lam felt oneness with the rock. The oneness told her the narrow, blue beam had penetrated two feet. Far enough. She released the trigger.

"Gelatine rod next," she called to Master Ye, and prayed the nitro glycerin in it wouldn't kill her.

"Send up gun, first," he shouted, as though he feared she would light today's fuses before the weapon-tool was safe.

Ting-Lam slid the gun into its canvas sack. Two tugs on the bag's lift rope and the device Ye had invented — one of many reasons he got paid better than the other railroad laborers from Southern China — ascended toward the top of the slope.

"Gun on its way," she called, so other workers above and below would know her progress.

Now for an explosive stick, the eighth and final one she would plant today. She slid the gelatine rod wrapped in crimson paper into the still-warm cavity within the mountain. Black powder — even dynamite — made her less nervous.

"May eight remain a lucky number and all eight sticks explode together." The wind played with the loose sleeves of her blue smock as she inserted a fuse cap around the rod's end.

"How much longer?" Ye shouted.

"After I walk circle."

Ting-Lam walked her tiniest *Baguachang* circle, a square comprised of four steps, really. As the hanging basket rocked, the toes on one foot practically touched the side of her other heel. Her palms faced her chest, as though she prepared to engage a human opponent in a sparring match, her long black hair braided in a queue and out of the way. Blasting gelatine mixed too strong had killed two of her people in a different tunnel yesterday.

Calmness. She must let that quality flow from her circular movement, from her breathing, the way she twisted her wrists with grace and cupped or flattened her palms. Yes, *Baguachang* facilitated the flow between body and mind.

Yet what was the purpose of Ting-Lam's body or mind anymore? A childless woman of twenty-six years won by Master Ye and pretending to be his nephew. She struck a match against granite, cupped her left hand and then lit the fuse. Death, like life, had its determined appointment. Sooner or later, all returned to emptiness. Some returned while they still lived.

"Fuse burns," she shouted upward.

"Beware," Master Ye bellowed from above, signaling to work crews with his arms. "Run."

Clanks of dropped shovels followed. Down the hillside below, workmen wearing straw hats scampered, water sloshing from their buckets. The fuse shortened as seconds passed, sizzling, lighting the companion fuses.

"Up, up," Ting-Lam yelled. "Hurry." What if the explosion killed her and the men discovered her woman's body? Such shame.

The basket inched upward. She must remain calm and steady. A woman of virtue accepted the inevitable but not without distress.

"Lock wrists with me," one of her Chinese comrades shouted.

He leaned over the precipice as the basket neared the top, clamping his dusty hands around her forearms. This was no time to let his touch bring a flush of embarrassment. She let him pull her free from the basket before it rested on firm ground. Then she ran with the men away from danger. Master Ye limped far ahead of them all, the moon-flame gun in his arms, his waist-length gray queue bobbing with his jerky movements.

The granite dragon roared. Stone spewed into the air like fireworks of angry giants. The heavens rained dirt, dust and gravel. Ting-Lam flattened herself against the rough earth, arms shielding her head, although the main blast shot away from her.

"Five feet," a man's voice shouted in Cantonese. "Maybe." He coughed. "To have certainty, we must clear this rubble."

Ting-Lam expelled air from her lungs. There was a chance, then, she would not have to work with that stronger and more dangerous blasting gelatine, the one that detonated with ease during mixing because of excess liquid nitro glycerin.

The aroma of black tea greeted Ting-Lam as she ladled the steaming beverage from the old powder keg into her earthenware teapot. Hundreds of Chinese laborers sat around the mountainside. Their chopsticks dipped into dented metal bowls filled with seaweed and rice.

"*Si*," one of the men whispered, gesturing in her direction.

He meant death. They thought she would be the next to die. But she need not endure their glances, for the cook's helper always brought her mid-day meal to Master Ye's shack. Both Ting-Lam and Ye must take advantage of the high sun's radiant warmth, return energy and natural balance to the crystal which powered the moon-flame gun.

Ting-Lam opened their shack's splintery door. The rusty iron hinges creaked, the welcoming sound of privacy. During the afternoon, she would continue helping Ye build a spare moon-flame gun. A better assignment than shoveling granite rubble until twilight. How fortunate they knew how to work with energized crystals. Still, Ye's moon-flame crystal held far more power than she could release, for she had not yet achieved true oneness with it. Her *qi* could flow across the crystal's surface but never filled the inside.

Sunlight streamed through a small glass window and onto a table where aligned lenses bathed in the nourishing rays. The circular black crystal, dark as a moonless midnight sky, rested beneath the lowest lens. Two bowls of rice and seaweed waited on the opposite end of the table. Master Ye sat cross-legged on a woven mat, his drooping mustache framing his lips. She poured tea and set his meal in front of him, then joined him on the floor.

"Do you think we conquered five feet?" Ting-Lam picked up her chopsticks and shoveled a lump of rice to her mouth.

"No matter," Ye said. "Brockton would find flaws in the Great Wall. Then want to rebuild it." A piece of seaweed dangled from the end of his chopsticks. "If we work in harmony, our current methods will suffice."

Ting-Lam sighed, preparing herself to receive yet another correction. "Is my work the flaw?"

"No," Ye said. "But we must look for a way to enlighten Brockton."

"Oh." Until she learned his weakness, a thousand candles wouldn't brighten that man.

"Besides," Ye added, "if we don't finish the main tunnels by winter, snow will finish many of us." He frowned, his facial creases more prominent than ever.

"But the company knows the danger of snow." Rough weather had forced them to suspend their tunnel building last winter.

"They've dropped too far behind schedule." Ye withdrew a pouch of dried herbs from the pocket of his robe. "I heard this morning they fear losing investment money and plan to push ahead regardless."

The barbarians dared challenge winter? Ting-Lam accepted the pinch of herbs Ye gave her and sprinkled it on her rice. The mixture that prevented her monthly bleeding brought bitterness to her tongue. Ye had emptied his tea cup. She reached for the pot.

"Tea can wait." How stern Master Ye sounded. "Walk the circle for me again. Always practice preparation for unwelcome surprises."

Ting-Lam had not finished her rice yet, but it would do no good to argue with Ye. When he decided it was time for a lesson in *Baguachang,* that was that. Did he think bandits waited to kidnap her? Or Brockton — who considered Buddha a devil — might attack? Best not to interfere with the replenishment of the delicate black crystal. Ye might sell her. She stood and moved well clear of both him and the table.

She bowed to him, then lowered a fist-sized stone from atop their covered clothes chest to the floor. Arms outstretched forward, elbows bent, curved palms facing the front of her shoulders. She walked with four small heel-to-toe steps around the stone. With each subsequent circle, she widened the distance between her and the stone, moving outward, her eyes surveying the one-room dwelling, inspecting even shadows.

Now she lifted her feet further off the ground when she stepped, her motions slow and graceful. *Baguachang* taught how to flow out of the way of harm, while using opponents' energy against them. Plus, in combat, a well-placed step, a knee in a precise location, could snap an opponent's leg bone in two pieces. Still less dangerous than blasting gelatine spiked with extra nitro glycerin. Oh, for a giant moon-flame beam to use instead of such unstable explosives.

"Lift your knees a little higher when you dragon step," Ye said. "Always keep your arms ready to protect your chest, throat and face."

Someday she would do this exercise to perfection, and Ye would offer praise instead of corrections. That would return a bit of her dignity. Besides, she had a duty to please him. He had once been a skilled master of this martial art before he injured his leg in a wagon accident. Not as skilled as Wu Sing would have been if *Baguachang* had existed back then.

Wu's skills included spreading harmony. Might he offer Ting-Lam advice about enlightening Brockton? Could Wu steal the energy from her emptiness? No, the path away from emptiness, like the path to achieve true oneness with the moon-flame crystal, must arise within her.

The sun slipped low in the western sky. The work gangs prepared to end their day. Ting-Lam's gang of twenty Chinese gathered outside on the mountain to hear the verdict. Had their crew of diggers and explosives handlers progressed five feet into the new tunnel today, or not?

The curly-headed Brockton climbed out of the lift basket, the quickest way to and from the excavation. His blue-gray eyes stared straight at Ting-Lam and the canvas sack containing the moon-flame gun. His meaty hand clutched a measuring stick. A frown formed on his round, bearded face. Not a good sign.

"Four feet, ten inches," Brockton announced.

Ting-Lam did not manage English well, but she understood measurements and the words ground into the pit of her stomach. Two inches short of the five-foot goal, the length of her little finger. The goal she had to reach to avoid premature explosions and more deaths.

"Two inches mean little to mountains." Hand grasping chin, Master Ye stepped forward. "I'll take my own measurement."

"So, I don't know what I'm doing, yer telling me?" Brockton said.

"No. Is the way of old men to see for themselves."

The moon-flame gun warmed Ting-Lam's hands through the heavy canvas sack, as though it invited her to achieve true oneness with its crystal. The wind whispered Cantonese words into her ear. A translation of Brockton's? Well, the barbarian's wishes were not inevitable. Wu Sing's were.

"Me go first," Ting-Lam said in English. She should explain herself, but English hurt her head and twisted her tongue. "Fix, fix." She stepped forward, pointed at the basket, then at the sinking sun. She turned toward Brockton. "Then you measure."

Master Ye squinted, accentuating the age lines on his face, his skin like wrinkled paper. Ye nodded. He trusted her to follow her own plan. Holding the moon-flame gun, she climbed into the empty lift basket. Her fellow workers lowered the woven vessel fifty feet down the mountainside as she put on her goggles.

At the landing, she set the canvas-wrapped gun on the floor of the bore, then climbed out. Not much light here. Night approached. Already someone raised the basket to carry Brockton down. Ting-Lam had better work fast. This trip, she would have no time for drawing Chinese characters.

She took several steps into the shadows. If Brockton focused on flaws, he could have made his tunnel-depth measurement on the most shallow section of the excavation. A bulge of earth, the width of her forearm, extended out from the rear wall of the excavation. Yes, this part was less deep. Could she obliterate two inches of granite here? She unpacked Master Ye's moon-flame gun, then raised the equipment to her shoulder.

Oh, spirit of Wu Sing. May the magic light work without the ritual just this once. She pulled the trigger. Nothing happened. Nothing! How foolish to set aside her ritual for the sake of speed. Now what was she going to do?

Then the silent blue light-beam streamed from the gun's barrel toward the bulge in the excavation's rear wall. Gray smoke rose, turning black and acrid. Thicker than ever before. She held her breath. Despite goggles, her stinging eyes teared. The beam had created as much smoke as an explosion. Blessed energy of Wu Sing. Coughing hard, she released the trigger. How much rock had she burned away?

A gust of wind thinned the smoke, revealing a huge hole where the bulge had been. She had not cut away a mere two inches of granite. More like two feet. A miracle!

"Servant of the devil!" The voice of Brockton Tim.

Ting-Lam wheeled around, pointing her gun toward the cavern floor. She hadn't understood all his words but knew the sounds of anger. Through shifting smoke, Brockton loomed tall near the tunnel's entrance, his canvas trousers and jacket coated with soot. If she and Brockton had stood back-to-back, the top of her head would not have reached his neck.

"I fix," she said. "You measure."

"Gimme that blasted thing," Brockton hollered.

He lunged toward Ting-Lam. She darted away from him with a dancing motion. Master Ye's gun must stay safe. She leaped toward the excavation's mouth and placed the moon-flame gun into the lift basket.

"Up," she shouted in Cantonese, pushing the basket clear of the tunnel even as she turned to confront Brockton.

"Heathen Chinaman!" His eyes glowered, brown-and-amber pools of rage. "'Tis sorcery yer after using to melt this much rock."

He dove at her again. Would he plunge them both down the steep slope?

With a sharp breath, Ting-Lam angled one of her feet so her heel met her toe. Her quick spiral, like a serpent's twist, moved her clear of Brockton's forward charge. A space waited behind the back of his heel. She aimed her foot toward there as she turned. The ground behind Brockton's foot met her own. He stumbled over her opposite leg and pitched forward.

"Sweet Jesus," Brockton shouted, as momentum thrust him in the direction of the precipice. But his death could never bring her harmony or dignity.

Her next forward twist delivered her in front of Brockton. Her shoulder slammed his chest. A whoosh of breath heaved from his lungs as Ting-Lam lurched away from him. Had she redirected his fall?

Ting-Lam turned to face Brockton. He lay on the floor of the tunnel. With a ragged groan, he pulled himself up, his curly hair like a mass of worms. He was safe. But now what? A voice whispered foreign words into her ear — English.

"Bad to fall off edge," she said, repeating what the voice had whispered, her arms still placed to guard her chest and throat, but shifting with serpentine motion.

Brockton just sat there, eyes wide as two teacups and his head angled to one side.

Why, she — Cho Ting-Lam — had won a match against granite and human stone. Teachers Wu and Ye had shown her the way but she had walked the path of discipline and discovered Brockton's weakness: unwelcomed surprise. Plus her qi had filled the crystal and summoned much energy from the moon-flame gun. Pleasant warmth spread through her.

Still, one task remained. Ting-Lam concentrated upon oneness with her surroundings. She could feel the barbarian's readiness to consider her terms. Perhaps a moon-flame woman's path to dignity depended neither on marriage nor sons.

"You. Me." Ting-Lam spoke using her deepest voice and bowed in Brockton's direction. The English words came easier now. "No more too much nitro. We build tunnel in harmony."

Brockton nodded in agreement and laughed, yet Ting-Lam felt his uncertainty. Foolish man. Enlightenment, like a patient mother, waited for his attention. He would learn.

KOMENAR Publishing released *Heroes Arise*, **Laurel Anne Hill**'s award-winning novel, in 2007. Her shorter works of fiction and nonfiction have appeared in a variety of publications. The fans of HorrorAddicts.net voted Laurel "Most Wicked 2011" for her steampunk/horror podcast, "Flight of Destiny."

Love and Rockets at the Siege of Peking

K. H. Vaughan

Bullets and shouts battered the walls of the British Consulate. Smoke from the burning shops and houses outside the lines of the foreign powers drifted everywhere, perturbed by shot and shell and the constant movement of the fire brigades. Ragged Chinese Christians carried water in soup tureens to prevent the flames from overrunning the 4000 souls within the legations. Outside, the Boxers ran through the streets with spears and knives screaming "*Sha! Sha!*"

Colonel Sir Claude Maxwell MacDonald, summoned to yet another urgent situation, paused to peer from an ersatz loophole. Corpses in the streets baked in the June sun. All the buildings around the diplomatic quarter were burning. Even the Hanlin Yuan library was not spared, although some of the diplomats had mounted a rescue attempt, crossing the alley under fire. A few books and artworks were recovered but most burned, including hundreds of Ming audio recordings on porcelain discs.

He considered the Boxers a disorganized rabble, suitable only for vandalizing railroads and butchering civilians. However, the ten-thousand Gansu Braves of General Dong Fuxiang were disciplined and carried modern Mausers. Their fire was withering and snipers continued to take a bloody toll.

"Well, Williams? What's all this then?" Sir Claude demanded, entering a stable the Welshman had converted to a workshop. The horses had long since been slaughtered for food.

"Sah!" Williams said, snapping to attention. "Mitchell here has got this machine cobbled together but she can't maneuver. What we need is a proper mechanic to sort it all out."

Sir Claude regarded the enormous crab-like monstrosity. The International Gun was an amalgam of scavenged parts, including a rusted iron cannon of uncertain origin with Russian shells of slightly wrong caliber, mounted on a baroque Italian motorized walking chassis, and powered by an American twin-piston Corliss engine. Even if the damned thing wouldn't fire it should scare the hell out of the attackers, clanking and scuttling about on its three hydraulic legs.

"You can man this thing?"

"Yes, Sir!" a Yank said, jumping down from the cockpit. "Gunner's Mate First Class, Joseph Mitchell, United States Marine Corp, Sir! I'm pretty handy with the Colt machine gun as well."

"Marine, eh? Embassy Guard? Damnedest thing, Navy men defending embassies."

"Sir, if this situation isn't like a ship repelling boarders I don't know what is."

"Quite," Sir Claude acknowledged. "Then the thing is to find a suitable mechanic, yes?"

"We've got plenty of men who can turn a spanner," Williams said. "But this…" He shook his head. He and Mitchell had been over the possibilities but had come up empty. The situation was grim.

"Perhaps I can be of assistance," came a cheerful voice. The American woman, Ann Margaret MacReedy, stood behind them in a heavy white linen shirt and canvas army trousers, her brilliant red hair pulled back.

"Madam! Whatever is it that you are wearing?" Sir Claude exclaimed.

"Trousers, Sir Claude," MacReedy said. "I'm sure you are familiar with them."

"Of course I am! However, this is highly irregular. Men's trousers? Not proper dress for a lady."

"I can't work in a dress, and the Boxers don't care if I wear a ball gown, trousers, or walk about in the altogether. Indeed, Miss Polly Condit Smith has taken to wearing her nightgown for that very reason. I'll not be hacked to pieces for propriety's sake."

The Colonel flushed and sputtered at MacReedy's suggestion and tried his gentlemanly best not to allow an image to form in his mind. Scandalous! No doubt a suffragette as well.

"Well, alright then," he concluded. "But what help can you possibly offer in this situation?"

"Mr. Williams? A Stillson wrench, please."

"Yes, mum!"

"Please, 'A.M.' or 'Morning,' or 'Miss MacReedy', if you cannot bring yourself to say either."

Morning MacReedy rolled up her sleeves and vanished to her waist within the gun's motion housing. After twenty minutes probing within she emerged, her face smeared with grease.

"It's not good, Mr. Williams," she said, sweeping aside a tendril of hair. "The piston valves are worn, there's a crack in the crosshead, and the lines are shot. We're losing a great deal of pressure between the boiler and the motive servos. We must have copper tubing."

"Well, mum, er ... Miss, you see, I'm afraid we haven't got any copper—" Williams began, then blanched with the realization.

"Surely it hasn't come to that yet?" he gasped.

"I'm afraid so," she said grimly. "We shall have to disassemble the distillery."

Williams groaned but Sir Claude waved him to it.

At dusk, MacReedy closed the housing and wiped sweat from her brow. "Those leather corset straps should hold. Bring it up to pressure. Mr. Williams, are the reach rods from the eccentrics to the valve mechanisms disconnected?"

"Yes, Miss!"

"Warm the cylinders. When she's ready, release the control rods and let the governor take over. Sir Claude — stand clear of that flywheel, please."

The machine coughed and sputtered, then gave way to a smooth rhythmic chugging, the dual walking beams plunging the pistons up and down evenly.

"Steady at one-hundred RPM," Mitchell called from the controls. "Pressure stable!"

"Very good, Mr. Mitchell!" MacReedy said. "Let's see if she'll move."

"Aye aye, Ma'am!" The marine began turning hand wheels and opening valves. He crossed himself, double clutched, and put the mechanism into gear. "C'mon, Betsey," he urged.

The International Gun blew a great cloud of steam from its cylinder cocks, and slowly rose on its three crablike legs. Mitchell traversed the cannon and the machine took several steps. He gave a thumbs-up. Soon the crump of the Russian shells joined the noise of the defenders' hodgepodge assortment of arms.

"Well done, A. M.," exclaimed Sir Claude, pumping her arm. "However did you learn to do such things?"

"My parents own a tool and die concern near Boston. I practically grew up in the machine shop."

"Three cheers for Morning MacReedy!" shouted Williams.

Only three months before, Morning MacReedy had accompanied several of the other American women in their finest silk gowns to a ball at the British Consulate. Polly Condit Smith leaned against a column in the ballroom, struggling to breathe in her corset of beaten copper, imported at great expense from France.

"That thing is ridiculous," MacReedy chided.

"It's the latest style," Polly gasped.

They took their champagne close to the lobby doors where Polly might get some air and were there when the Chinese delegation arrived.

"That fellow is quite handsome, don't you think?" MacReedy said, casting her gaze upon a tall man in the formal uniform of a Captain of the Imperial Guard. "What a striking figure."

"Perhaps," Polly said. "For an Oriental."

"You are unkind!"

"Then I dare you to dance with him."

MacCreedy hesitated. Polly grinned mischievously, and MacCreedy knew she had lost.

"Excuse me, then," she said, and made her way across the floor, leaving Polly's giggles behind.

"Good evening, I…" she faltered, for she spoke little Chinese. She knew this would happen. Oh, Polly had put her in it! One of the men said something in Mandarin and a number of them laughed. The Captain bowed and extended his hand.

"If it will help, I speak English," he said and they stepped comfortably into the string quartet's waltz.

"Li-Quiang Ping of the Imperial Guard," he said.

"Ann Margaret MacCreedy with the American consulate."

They danced and talked without pause into the late evening, and all else fell away from them. Polly was scandalized, which only added to MacReedy's pleasure. As they danced, drifting among the other guests, bits and pieces of conversation about the Boxers intruded. Demonstrations. Missionaries and converts massacred in the countryside. Trains and merchant goods burned.

She did not wish to spoil the mood of the encounter, but she couldn't ignore what she knew they both heard.

"What is your opinion of the unrest in the countryside?"

"Many are concerned about foreign influences and intentions," he said carefully. "They call themselves the *I-ho ch'üan*, the 'Society of Righteous and Harmonious Fists.' Your colleagues have a name for them that I am unfamiliar with."

"Yes, 'Boxers'. We have no martial arts of your kind, so to call a man who trains to fight bare-handed a boxer respects him as something other than a common brawler."

"Ah, but does China have the respect of the Western powers?"

"I would think that East and West have a great deal to offer one another."

"Perhaps as individuals," he smiled. "It is not my place to have a position on foreign policy. My loyalty belongs solely to the Empress."

There was a commotion in the street and much shouting. The music stopped and people went to the windows to peer outside.

Rough men walked through the streets in small groups, their queues tied in red cloth and red ribbons on their wrists and ankles. They carried banners and were armed with spears and knives. They were screaming "*Sha! Sha!*"

"What are they saying?" MacReedy whispered.

"They are saying 'Kill!'" Ping said. "'Kill the foreign devils.'"

Imperial troops restored calm and the Boxers were sent outside the city. Ping and MacReedy saw one another as often as possible in the next weeks, strolling happily through the plazas in the city. She rode in the sidecar of his steam-powered velocipede, and repaired the Stephenson linkage with a hairpin and rubber band when it broke down.

It grew increasingly difficult to see one another. The army was unwilling or unable to prevent demonstrations and riots, and Ping was restricted more and more to the Forbidden City. The last time they saw each other before the siege, they picnicked among the clockwork zodiac animals outside the Temple of Heaven in Tiantan Park.

The Boxers burned down the club at the racetrack and dragged Chancellor Sugiyama in his top hat and tailcoat from his carriage and hacked him to death in the street. Children danced and poked the corpse with sticks. The legations were reinforced with 400 troops from the coast. Finally, Manchu officers shot Baron von Ketteler on his way to the foreign ministry, and all pretense that the Empress Dowager wished to prevent violence was lost. Soon after, the legations were surrounded and the population within swelled with Chinese Christians fleeing massacre.

The siege had begun.

"I am prepared to address the Ministers," announced the Empress Dowager Cixi in her personal chambers beneath the audience hall in the Imperial Palace. She sat upon the Dragon Throne, eyes fixed on her hologram of Queen Victoria as an intricate glass dome was lowered over the throne and secured. Sealed within, she was surrounded by a Faraday cage of the most exquisite copper thread embedded within the surface of the glass.

Ping stood to the front of the Empress Dowager's dais in the hall above, prepared to draw his sword at any moment. His eyes searched for threats among the two thousand assembled generals and officials. The provincial magistrates were, at best, under nominal control and a warlord like General Dong Fuxiang was at the edge of open defiance. His personal guards were stripped of weapons but were formidable warriors even open-handed. Ping suspected that they had additional arms hidden upon their persons; various gears and rods within their armored carapaces seemed sharper than needed for their pure mechanical function. The Imperial Guard danced a complex diplomatic dance in their efforts to protect the Empress Dowager, even within her own court.

The ministers themselves were arrayed on the floor before the dais according to rank and influence. Each brain floated in a glass jar decorated with sacred animals, each repository ornate in proportion to the occupant's status. The most ancient were relegated to the shelves lining the walls of the perimeter, their pallid cortices atrophied, their jars collecting dust. The jars buzzed, exchanging tense whispers through speaker grills. The week prior she had ordered several of the liberal ministers smashed upon the floor.

The enormous chamber grew silent as the Empress Dowager's hyperbaric dome rose up through the floor. Behind her was a device with the appearance of an impossibly complex pipe organ, and attendant eunuchs scurried to attach hoses to fittings. Commissioned from the Australian firm of Fincham and Sons, it fed a stream of incense, perfume, and opium into her chamber.

Taoist monks evaluated her qi and adjusted the blend according to their alchemies.

The Empress Dowager spoke.

"We cannot consent to the incursions of the Westerners and their ideas. They would carve China up among themselves. Even if we prevent this, some virulent ideological notion from Europe or America may infect the people and it will be the end of our culture and of Manchu rule."

Her mask was a complicated array of cylinders and lenses that gave her the appearance of a spider with its many eyes. It clicked and whirred quietly as lenses swapped in and out to magnify or shrink objects within her sight, or to change a variety of colored filters.

"We must employ all our powers in defense of the Qing Dynasty," her voice thundered from columns of speaker stacks. "Let the army take control of the Society of Fists. We declare war against all foreign powers."

General Dong scowled with pleasure and Ping's heart ached, but of his pain he permitted no sign. The ministers buzzed and hissed their staticky approval from within their dusty jars.

A barrage of fireworks illuminated the rubble and charred timbers surrounding the legations. Constant gunfire harassed the besieged. Within the compound, Morning MacReedy sat in an open court-yard and watched the colorful bursts. It had been a long day spent repairing the water jacket on the Austrian Maxim gun. Afterwards, she had cut bandages from petticoats and helped fill sandbags sewn from curtains. The stench of smoke and of the unburied dead hung heavily in the air.

Sir Claude emerged. He had been a lean man before the siege began, and was leaner still after weeks of rice and scant pony meat.

"Champagne?" she offered. There was little water but there were still cases of the stuff.

"We've managed a fine defense," he said as he joined her.

"No need to put on a good face on my account. The army seems content to volley rifle fire when they could overrun us. They send Boxers piecemeal with scavenged weapons and joss sticks to slaughter against the barricades. A focused bombard-ment and their cannon would transmogrify the whole district to dust and tears."

Sir Claude almost continued his effort to comfort her but thought better of it. He stroked his mustache, which he kept neat, but the mustache wax had run out. A trifle, but sometimes it was the little things that a man noticed.

"I must confess, I didn't know what to make of you at first," he said. "No matter the outcome, it has been an honor to have served with you."

"Thank you Sir Claude. I feel the same."

They toasted as the Maxim gave forth another staccato burst and rockets shrieked through the August night.

The Empress Dowager Cixi sat in her chambers upon the Dragon Throne. Without her mask, her eyes were brown and her face worn with fatigue and age. She watched as the Imperial Scholars frantically fed memorials into her *qílín's* dragon mouth. It was impossible to keep up, and most were simply burned unanalyzed. The wheels and gears within the gold-scaled torso hummed and the engine scribed predictions with its tail upon scrolls. The *qílín* was kept under constant guard, lest members of the court sabotage its calculations.

"Captain Li-Quiang Ping," she said. "I have been manipulated and misled about our enemy's strength and intentions, and now we face grave danger. The Eight-Nation Alliance has sent a relief column from Tianjin. Even now they approach our walls. I will order the evacuation of the Forbidden City and instruct the army to lift the siege, but General Dong is strongly against the foreigners. He will seek to cause whatever harm he can."

"I shall prepare for the evacuation," Ping said.

She shook her head.

"I know that people think me very hard, and it is true. But I remember love," she smiled. "Did you think I did not know? Protect her, Li-Quiang Ping. See that she is safe from Dong Fuxiang's assassins until her countrymen arrive, and then return to defend us against our enemies both without and within our palace."

The shells fell heavily as Morning MacReedy ran to the American barricades atop the Tartar Wall with her tool belt. Massive stone fortifications surrounded Peking and the small section directly overlooking the legations had been held by a small contingent of Germans and Americans, separated from the Chinese by makeshift barricades.

"That two-pounder is murder!" shouted a private after a shell smashed into the wall below, jarring their teeth. "We'll all be killed!"

"It's their last chance to overwhelm us before the relief column arrives. We've got to hold on!" she urged.

Another shell exploded on the wall close by and MacReedy shielded the exposed workings of the Colt with her body from the debris. When the dust had settled she reconnected the gas piston to the retraction mechanism with sewing machine parts. She tested the repair and the machinegun's action cycled smoothly.

"That's got it!" she shouted, and watched anxiously as the soldiers fed a fresh belt of ammunition and began firing on the Chinese cannon emplacement.

"We need more ammunition," the sergeant yelled. "Six millimeter!"

"I'll see what I can do," she said, and made her way back to the ramp leading down into the diplomatic quarter. Bullets hissed through the air and smacked off the stone around her. She could hear the sound of bugles and bagpipes drifting in the distance. The relief force was approaching.

She caught movement in the corner of her eye. Dong Fuxiang's personal guard swooped through the air on wings of black silk, leather, and bamboo, silently in the evening sky, illuminated by the fires below. They set upon the German barricade, and soldiers screamed and fell beneath a fusillade of magazine-fed darts. More approached the American barricade behind her. She screamed a warning but they could not hear over the bombardment and the hammering of the Colt. She ran toward them drawing her semi-automatic and fired at the assassins. Two fell, but a third discharged a static bolt gun and the soldiers collapsed in a smoking heap.

MacReedy paused to reload when she heard a sound behind her. She turned and confronted one of the Gansu. This was no Boxer peasant believing himself magically protected from bullets, but a deliberate killer in armor both elaborate and malignly functional. He raised his arm, on which was mounted a brass hand cannon on mechanical shock absorbers. The assassin sneered, and as she scrambled to replace her magazine she found herself marveling at the cannon's bore, which must have been at least 35 mm.

"You would be thinking of the engineering at a time like this, wouldn't you?" she thought as she realized that he would shoot first.

In the moment when he should have fired, an arrow lodged in the barrel and his arm exploded in a shower of rods and gears.

She looked back.

Ping stood beyond the barricade atop the Tung Pien gate, bow in hand. He ran down the side of the tower, leaping from gable to gable in majestic strides, then over the downed Americans toward his countrymen. His sword sliced easily through a Gansu, who fell in a spray of blood, wheels, and springs. MacReedy slapped her magazine home and opened fire, her rounds slamming another assassin back between the crenellations and over the wall. In the space of moments, they stood alone, untouched by the gunfire all around them.

"You're safe, my lady," Ping said, sheathing his sword.

"You came for me."

"I could do nothing else," he said, touching her soot-stained cheek.

There was a loud roar, and they were joined by an American soldier in a forced-steam jetpack, who landed atop the wall in a billowing cloud. He pulled back his goggles to reveal the youthful face beneath.

"Calvin P. Titus, Corporal, United States Army, Ma'am. We're here to rescue you," he said, and all three exchanged handshakes.

"Duty demands that I return to the Empress," Ping said sadly.

"I know. Will I ever see you again?"

"Who can say in these times?"

They kissed, for the first and last time, and the entire city shook. With a thunderous rumble the Imperial Palace began to rise, a massive cloud washing over the Forbidden City and Peking.

"Fellah, I believe your ride is leaving," Titus said. "I guess maybe you better borrow this contraption." He shrugged the leather harness from his shoulders and extended the jetpack to Ping.

"You are generous to an officer of your enemy," Ping said.

"Enemy?" Titus winked. "Well, then I guess I must have mistaken you for somebody else."

Ping flew away and Morning watched long after he vanished somewhere into the pagodas of the Imperial Palace. Bursts of fire reflected off the golden roof and pink walls as it gained altitude, massive vents below belching smoke and flame. It yawed slightly, and slowly accelerated to the west, fleeing the British gunships floating over the horizon toward them.

She knew that she would never see him again.

In his other life, **K. H. Vaughan** is a Ph.D. in Clinical Psychology and refugee from academia who has taught, published, and presented professionally on a variety of topics, most related to forensic psychology and methodology. An avid sports fan, he is past chair of the Science Committee for the Society of American Baseball Researchers. He lives in New England with his wife and three children.

The Master and the Guest

Crystal Koo

They sit under the brown tarp as the caravan shakes from the dirt rocks underneath. The conversation earlier, made tepid by their shock, has died into a murky, distracted silence.

This is his first time trying to sleep in a body physically not able to. Wood for muscle, steel for bone. The events of the last few days pass behind his shuttered eyelids. Memories leave their places and come scraping toward him, separated only by thin lights that wave back and forth. His skin being shred off, his bones dislocated, his organs imploding, smoke filling every cavity in his body. Ribbons of tendons snap and muscle comes off in strips, swathes of nerves tear away from his spine, and somewhere in the back, the sound of forge welding. Below the sound of someone's screams, a hammering like a low-voiced, workman's chatter. Interrupted sensations — pain, the blackness of hatred, his terror — hang in the charged air, phantoms of his breath, his energy, flowing from his butchered carcass to the wooden coffin they've prepared for him, one conduit to another.

Everything fades and flashes. The caravan lurches around a bend.

On the other side of town, opposite the direction of where the train is heading, a man in a cramped room bends over a feverish woman and places a wet towel on her forehead.

Much of the beige paint on the man's face had been scraped off, revealing patches of startling, translucent white underneath. The colors made him look like a ravaged doll. His queue had been shorn off — in defiance of the emperor? An accident? — and he wore his ragged hair down to his shoulders. His infantryman's uniform had been reduced to green tatters and did a very bad job of concealing the willowleaf sword sheathed below his belt.

One of the servant's sons brought him to the yard in the center of the courtyard. The master sat in front of a small table, painting the clothes of a fisherman chiseled on sandalwood. A few rough figurines were on the table. The master gave a small, unpainted sparrow to the boy, who clutched it and grinned up and down the soldier's sword until the master told the boy to return to his mother.

"You looked for me," said the master.

"I looked for everyone," answered the guest. "Am I interrupting your work?"

"I don't make these to sell anymore." The master removed his glasses. "We should move to the study." He collected the brushes, putting them tips first into a little jar of water. Colors bloomed like a swarm of jellyfish.

"You shouldn't let them soak too much," said the guest.

"We won't be long," said the master. "Anyway they won't be much use to me when we finish."

The guest followed the master through moon gates and verandahs to the northernmost, most private side of the complex. The sounds of vendors and children from the street receded, muffled by the layers of neat, private gardens in the courtyard. The master opened the wooden lattice doors to the study.

"You've done well for yourself," said the guest as the master lit the lamps.

The study was clean and tidy. On one wall hung a small portrait of a young woman with a high forehead. Writing instruments were arranged by function on the desk and finished figurines lined a shelf against the wall. Opera characters carved in wood and ivory — the clown, the concubine, the arrogant monkey, the general, the fire-spitting prince. All thirty pieces had a small mask painted in bright colors.

"Northern and southern varieties," said the guest, looking at the green-faced prince holding butterfly knives and spitting fire from his mouth. "You travel often?"

"I did. Not so much now." The master sat on the chair behind the desk. There was no other chair. The guest indicated with his hand that he preferred to stand anyway. "How have you been?" asked the master.

The guest told him of his own travels. A trip to the closest barracks in the province for preliminary training, then a convoy to the capital for more training, examinations, and his formal induction into the imperial army. Then a long trek past the sand dunes of the Gobi, across Mongolia where he spent some years in campaigns to quell local uprisings, and finally the outpost at the nebulous border in Siberia.

"Mr. Ying traveled a great deal too," said the guest.

"The sign of a successful merchant."

"You went with him?"

"No, I never saw him again. Well, that's not true, I went to his funeral two weeks ago. I left early, it was too crowded." The master adjusted his tone to keep it light. "But between that and the last time you and I saw each other, never again."

"I was at the funeral as well. I saw you and followed you home."

The master didn't answer.

"You look well," said the guest. "I heard that you used to live in a small room above a teahouse, next to a family of nightsoil collectors. You had a girl too." He pointed at the portrait. "I'm envious. Some rebels in Ulanhot, they didn't understand us. They thought they could buy time with their women and threw a bunch of whores our way. We had to slaughter everyone. This woman is your wife?"

"She was never my wife. Not the marrying kind."

"How is she?"

"She died of malaria close to when you left."

"I'm sorry."

The master could tell he didn't mean it.

"That was before," said the guest. "Now you have the biggest courtyard in town, you say you carve only for pleasure, and you're getting round in the waist."

The master allowed a difficult smile. "I was younger then. I could work without eating or sleeping."

"Or without a conscience." The guest unrolled the remains of his left sleeve up to his shoulder. "You only have small pieces on display here. Where do you put the big ones? Aside from the army barracks, I mean."

The master stared at his own surname etched on the steel ball of the guest's shoulder. The tail of the right sign of the ideogram was jagged, a groove improperly done.

The master remembered which one this particular guest was now. Ten years ago, under the bad light of Mr. Ying's lanterns, the master had been pushing a graver against a steel ball to create the last curve of his own name when Mr. Liu had finished the energy transfer. The moment Mr. Liu lifted his hands from the corpse and the wooden doll, the doll had woken up. A scream crackled in his voice box and the doll had wrenched himself away.

It had been the first time the master had seen a doll animated. He had dropped the graver.

The guest saw that he recognized him. "Mr. Liu had to withdraw some of my energy to keep me down. You were looking at me the whole time. I remember you looking as lean and as rabid as a gurkha. You were terrified of me. You started blithering like an idiot, about how you were doing it for her." The guest pointed at the portrait of the young woman.

"I couldn't afford her doctors then. The money I got paid with after was solely for that," the master said. "To not have taken advantage of everything I was capable of to save her life would've been to have no conscience."

"When you told me earlier that she had died, you sounded like you were telling someone else's story. As though it had meant nothing to you or that she wasn't worth remembering." The guest's face was a wooden impasse. "That's not very convincing."

"I remember her every day. That's all I've done for the past ten years."

"You look too well-adjusted for that."

"Don't lecture me about sorrow. It's a terrible thing but one must learn to let it pass."

"Because you think I know nothing about it. Because the next thing I knew when I woke up, I was on a caravan on its way to the barracks, remembering how I begged you to save me and all you said was that you had to save her, this girl I couldn't even see. I could see my human body turned inside out and this girl whom you had coerced me to save I couldn't even see."

The guest had gone absolutely still. In the study, he looked like the master's most lifelike sculpture. "Explain to me, please," he said, "how it's possible that you did nothing. That you continued what Mr. Ying told you to do."

"She was dying."

"You think we didn't die? They couldn't kill us in the battlefield because we were already dead. We were thirty boys that Mr. Ying's men had smoked out from the opera troupe house so you and Mr. Liu could turn us into this. So Mr. Ying could sell us to the emperor and put his sons in the mandarin hall."

"You don't understand."

"Explain to me and I will." The guest waved at the shelf of thirty opera figurines. "Because it's not enough. A tribute to the dead isn't enough. The townspeople say you're a philanthropist. They love you, though they don't know where you got the money and they don't know why you put so much effort to open orphanages. I know the answers to that and it's not enough."

"I couldn't turn back once we had started," the master said. "I didn't want to do it. It was just a job."

"I said the same to each Mongolian who had time to plead for his life but it never made a difference to the widows and children they had left behind. It's only fitting that at the end of the day, you couldn't save your woman. Your sin had killed her."

"Stop it."

"You've thought the same for the past ten years."

"That's not true."

"You had a chance and you chose wrongly. You left me on that table, you left all of us there, and because of that she's dead."

"I want you to leave now."

"That's why you try to atone yourself with these little figurines and your little orphanages, thinking if you could make us come to life again, somehow she'll come to life too."

The master was silent.

"If you had to live your life one more time, would you do it again?"

The guest carefully moved the brushes and the inkstones from one side of the table and perched on it.

"You would," said the guest, "and I'd ask why and you'd say I know nothing about love. I wonder whose fault that is."

The master looks at the jade pieces inset above the guest's nose, eyes that would never rest behind closed eyelids. He had known it earlier, but now with the fullness of understanding, he thought: I will be killed in my own house, surrounded by ghosts.

The guest was hunched over, studying the blue face of a small concubine.

The master wanted to talk to him about fear, not for one's life but for someone else's. He wanted him to hear the internal scream in a person watching someone he loved being carried away by the tide inches away from his face while his hands were tied behind his back. The blindness that blacked out everything else. In those lean days, there was only the room above the teahouse, her body convulsing under the blanket, the walls letting the cold air in like an open window, the vomit on the floor. How could thirty opera troupe boys who were given the chance to never die compare? But after the money came, it was the same thing, only with nightmares. He had dreamed that she had turned into wood after a fit and he was scorching his name on her shoulder.

The guest was talking about the other men he had visited before coming to the master's courtyard. Mr. Liu. Mr. Ying. Mr. Liu's son was good with a halberd and had chopped his hair off. Mr. Liu's son had tried hard.

The master was not listening. He was thinking of the time Mr. Liu offered to transfer what was left of her spirit into another wooden doll if he wanted and he had refused. He had remembered how the newly-awakened soldiers had reacted, as though they knew there would never be peace in a wooden body, and after all that fighting perhaps she deserved that peace. He could not give a name to what he had felt when she died. It was not grief. It was the floating sensation between losing your footing and falling into an infinite darkness. He had hung in the air for years.

"You're crying," said the guest. "We can use some music. Maybe I can show you some of the things I used to do before."

The guest went to the door and went outside. The master heard him calling loudly for the servants to bring someone who could play something cheerful for the master.

When the guest returned, he pulled the willowleaf sword out of its sheath. The master knew there was nothing else to understand about each other. But despite the calm in his mind, he wet himself under his robes as he watched the blade draw nearer.

"You know this is right," the guest said. "The world plays many tricks on us. For all of us who can't fulfill our own plans for greatness, to be able to do the right thing is more than enough. This sword is for you."

"Please."

"Listen to me. Don't cry. I'm being fair. I won't have you defend yourself without a weapon."

The master sagged against his seat. The ammoniac odor of urine rose in the room. The guest took the sword, his hand closing over the blade unscathed, and handed it to the master, hilt first.

The master refused it.

"If it pleases you." The guest placed the sword on the table and grasped the master's neck. His fingers were cold and he began squeezing the master's neck with a precise, mechanical gradation of strength.

A knock on the door, timid and quavering, almost as if someone had been peeking through the lattice and had seen what was happening.

The guest let go and the master fell from the chair, sobbing. The guest opened the door. A servant girl held a lute in her arms and she stared at him, lips pale.

For a moment they stood in a triangle, the master on the floor, the guest by the door, and the servant girl on the verandah, all knowing that the roles had now been switched: the servant on the floor, the master by the door, and the guest on the verandah.

"Your master would like some music," said the guest as the master struggled to return to the chair. "Please."

The girl caught the urine smell and gasped. She began crying when she saw the sword on the table and the purple bruise marks around the master's neck.

"Play," said the guest.

The girl did, with trembling fingers, and did it very badly. The guest listened intently. The girl stared at the floor as her fingers played more wrong notes on the lute.

The guest knew the folksong she was playing. He hummed along; his voice box made a sound like the rasping of a metal grate. Then he drew the sword from the table.

He twisted his wrist, pantomiming the movements of the opera. He brandished the sword in slow, large arcs and lifted his legs with the music, dancing with the cruel innocence of a boy pretending to be a soldier. He sang about a young man climbing up a tree to pick nuts and a woman below with the basket calling him to come home. The mountain is beautiful, the river long, the sun is setting, and the birds have returned, come home, come home.

The lute slipped from the girl's hands. The master looked at the portrait.

Ten minutes later, the guest left the study, the sword swinging by his hip. He returned to the yard where the master's brushes were soaking in the jar of water. The guest took them out, smoothing the rabbit hair the best he could with his wooden fingers, and hung them on the cherry-colored brush rack to dry.

Crystal Koo was born and raised in Manila and is working in Hong Kong. Her latest publications are or are forthcoming in venues such as Abyss & Apex, Lauriat, Philippine Speculative Fiction 7, and The World SF Blog. She is currently writing a script for a graphic novel.

Ming Jie and the Coffee Maker of Doom

Brent Nichols

Meng Jie stepped into the kitchen of Gearfalcon Manor, heart thumping, fighting for calm. He had endured the harsh training of the Granite Palm Brotherhood and fought the assassins of the Black Dragon Gang, but he had not known true fear until he faced a modern coffee machine.

He stared up at the gleaming mass of copper and steel. What eight hundred pounds of spinning gears and surging steam did that a hand-cranked grinder and a coffee pot couldn't do was beyond Meng, but working for the world's greatest inventor meant that life contained certain challenges.

The machine had no fewer than seventeen brass levers on the front, none of them labelled. A mistake could mean far more than a bad cup of coffee. Carter never did anything on a small scale. This machine had enough power to destroy the house.

Meng scowled and pulled the master pressure lever. Instead of sending their finest assassins after Carter, the Black Dragon Gang should drop by for a chat and ask for a cup of coffee. Sooner or later that would do the trick.

The machine rumbled and Meng pulled several levers, bleeding off pressure into the secondary systems. The rumbling subsided, gears whirred, and Meng stepped back. The mechanical monstrosity deserved his unwavering attention, but he had other, equally pressing duties.

He stepped into the corridor, closed the kitchen door, and listened. He heard the faint murmur of voices from Carter and his guests in the library. Beyond that, silence.

Was that the hint of a breeze on his skin? Meng crept down the hall and peered into the drawing room. A window was open, a figure in black just wriggling under the sash. Meng sprang forward, snatched up an ashtray, and clipped the intruder smartly under the ear. The black-clad body went limp.

Meng left the assassin snoring and locked in a closet and headed back toward the kitchen, then paused outside the library door, listening.

The smug, plummy voice of Lord Havisham said, "Two million pounds. My final offer absolutely."

Carter, his Canadian accent contrasting with the clipped British diction of his guests, said, "That's very generous, but—"

"What are the Chinese paying you?" Sir Henry interrupted. "Something in the range of a hundred thousand dollars, I hear. You can't pass up two million pounds for that."

"Well, you see, I—"

"I don't think you're seeing the big picture," said Havisham. "Do you have any idea how important the opium trade is to the empire? Your airships are sailing right over our naval blockade. You're making a joke of the Royal Navy! Come now, sir! If you won't act from personal interest, think of your patriotic duty!"

"I would love to help you," Carter said. "But I can't break my agreement with Peking. You see, we shook hands."

Meng trotted back to the kitchen, smiling. Carter could be incredibly exasperating, and he seemed to have less common sense than a rock lobster. Meng had thwarted five different assassination attempts, and Carter still thought he was nothing more than a butler. But Carter would keep his word in the face of massive bribes and mortal peril, and Meng loved him for it.

The entire kitchen was trembling by the time he arrived, and Meng frantically drained off steam. When the worst of the danger was past he grabbed a cup and eyed the spigot below the machine. If too much pressure remained, the coffee would erupt with the force of a flying back-kick. There were marks on the opposite wall to prove it.

Meng held his breath and eased the spigot open. A dribble of dark fluid leaked out, and he wrinkled his nose at the burned smell. He flushed the pipes and started over. The machine trembled as the pressure built, a light sweat sprang out on Meng's forehead, and he muttered, "They better be damned thirsty."

The front door creaked and Meng hurried into the hall. The Englishmen were putting on their hats, Havisham's whiskers bristling indignantly beneath his red cheeks. "You're making a mistake, Carter," he snapped, and stomped out. Sir Henry was a sleek shape in pinstripes scurrying in his wake.

Wilson, the youngest of the Englishmen, hung back. Wilson and Carter were superficially similar, tall, clear-eyed men in their thirties. But Wilson was every inch the businessman, with a tailored suit and plump, soft hands. Carter was in his shirt-sleeves, and his broad shoulders, plus a smear of grease unnoticed beneath his left eye, spoke of the time he spent in his workshop.

Wilson fiddled with his hat. "Mr. Carter? I'm sorry to bother you after you've given your answer. It's just... My family fortune is on the line, you see. The last of my capital is tied up in opium, and this Chinese ban is killing me. I know they'll capitulate if you withdraw your airships."

His face was twisted by shame and desperation. "As a personal favour, to a man who's about to lose everything, will you help me?"

Carter murmured, "I wish I could." His gaze lifted, he saw Meng, and he smiled. "Well, at least you can have a cup of coffee before you go. Is it ready, Meng? Did you remember the milk?" Carter turned to Wilson. "He always forgets the milk."

Wilson jammed on his hat and stalked out. Carter looked at Meng, shrugged, and said, "Never mind the coffee, I guess."

Meng turned back toward the kitchen. The pressure would be rising to dangerous levels by now. Then his feet slowed, and he frowned. His instincts were telling him there was a danger even greater than the coffee maker, but from where?

It was Wilson, he realized. Wilson's face had shown not just desperation but a terrible resolve.

The front door crashed open and Wilson stood there, wild-eyed, with a strange contraption strapped to his back. There were brass cylinders, leather straps, gears and knobs and dials, and for an awful moment Meng thought he was going to brew coffee. Then he saw the tubes running up Wilson's arm, the brass cuff, the barbed points of half a dozen metal darts.

"What the—" Carter stood frozen in the doorway of the library, and Wilson snarled and pointed his arm. Three steel darts shot from his wrist cuff, straight at Carter.

Meng sprang into action, snatching the darts from the air in mid-flight. Then he shoved Carter backward, sending him stumbling into the library.

Wilson snarled and touched his wrist. A jet of hot steam shot out, and Meng flinched back. Wilson advanced, his snarl changing to a grim smile. Each time Meng tried to approach, Wilson drove him back with a jet of steam. Meng looked around, frantic, and darted into the kitchen. Wilson followed, implacable.

Meng shot a glance at the coffee maker. The main pressure gauge was scarlet. If he didn't take care of Wilson soon, all three of them would be blown to Kingdom Come.

Wilson strode forward, firing gouts of steam with every step. Meng snatched up a bowl of oranges, threw one, and nailed Wilson on the forehead. That wiped the man's smile away, but only for a moment.

Meng threw the next orange at the wrist cuff, hoping to clog the jet, but the orange was impaled on the barbs of the remaining darts. The next blast of steam vaporized the orange, filling the room with a citrus smell.

Wilson took another step, coming even with the coffee spigot, and Meng threw his final orange. He banked it off of the milk pressure valve and hit the spigot handle.

Every ounce of pressure in the machine released in one terrible, chicory-scented jet. A blast of dark fluid slammed into the contraption on Wilson's back, spinning him around and knocking him to the floor. Coffee sprayed the far wall in a torrent that quickly slowed to a dribble, then stopped.

Carter peered in through the kitchen doorway, then stepped inside. He was pale with shock, but he grinned and said, "Someone finally had coffee, I see." Wilson struggled into a sitting position, and Carter picked up a milk bottle from the counter and thumped the would-be killer over the head. Wilson slumped, and Carter said, "Meng, you always forget the milk."

Meng sagged onto a stool, spent, as Carter surveyed the devastation in the kitchen. "Meng," he said, "it's not that I'm not grateful. You saved my life, after all. Still, this coffee maker is a delicate piece of machinery, and I wish you would treat it with more care."

He looked down at Wilson. "Just keep an eye on our guest for a moment while I put in a call to the police. I suppose we better tie him up. Oh, I'll have to ask you to tidy up the kitchen a bit, as well." He pursed his lips. "It seems like a lot of bother, when there's all this steam power right here. I wonder if I could design something that would…"

He wandered out, still mumbling, and Meng shook his head, stepped over Wilson's unconscious form, and went to get a mop.

Brent Nichols is a notorious mad scientist who builds steam-powered doomsday devices in a secret lair deep beneath the city of Calgary. He also teaches software courses and writes lurid tales of fantasy and science fiction. His wife Tammy is his biggest source of inspiration.

A Hero Faces the Celestial Empire; A Death by Fire is Avenged by Water

Julia A. Rosenthal

Ai Ouyang, Hero of Eight Rat Mountain, supreme genius of steel and fire, was at the end of his patience with the woman on the train tracks.

She sat cross-legged. Her knees, hidden beneath the pale purple silk of her embroidered trousers, rested on the steel rails of the narrow-gauge tracks. The rails were burnished to a gleam by the wheels of steam engines that rolled over the metal at twenty-five miles per hour, six times a day. Her hands were curled around the rails as if she were about to lift herself out of a sedan chair.

The woman faced south, toward Shanghai Station and the Celestial Empire, which was due in — Ai Ouyang reached into his surcoat and pulled out his brass pocket watch — eleven minutes.

"I have a grievance," the woman said. Her eyes were fixed on a point far down the tracks.

Ai Ouyang leaned over, took a deep hero's breath and addressed the single jade bead hanging from a gold clasp at her earlobe.

"Honorable Lady," he said, "you managed to send word to me at the teahouse. Couldn't we have met there?"

The woman said nothing.

A fragment of cloud drifted across the sun. The breeze, which still carried an edge of April-morning chill, stirred the white flowers growing along the tracks.

Ai Ouyang listened through the whispering of the breeze for the approaching train. He heard only the foreign concessions surrounding the train line: the thudding of horses' hooves pulling carts through the muddy streets, the calls of street vendors in Shanghainese and English, and the laughter and shouts of children running past on the other side of the stone wall that followed the tracks.

"I have a grievance, Hero Ai."

Ai Ouyang glared.

He stepped between the steel rails and crouched before the woman. The words of his teacher, Master Hu Guofan, the Seven-Clawed Tiger, echoed in Ai Ouyang's ears:

Never turn your back on your enemy.

He looked over his shoulder. No train coming.

"In the stories," Ai Ouyang said, "people bring their grievances *to* the heroes." He turned back to the woman, who was now looking at him. Her eyes, though set in a face no older than sixteen, had a quiet sorrow that he had seen in grandmothers mourning the loss of entire families. "Yet you, Honorable Lady, asked me to meet you out here. Why? We could have discussed this at the teahouse."

The woman's mouth pressed into a thin line before she spoke. "Yes, Hero Ai. I could have met you anywhere. But I needed you to understand how my brother died." Her chin lowered. Ai Ouyang had to lean forward to hear her speak. "He was walking here — it was back in August — and a train came. It struck him. It — his head was — he died right away."

"Right here?" Ai Ouyang asked.

The woman nodded.

"I remember this. I saw it in the newspapers."

"Yes. The newspapers. They called my brother a lunatic."

"Well…" Ai Ouyang started to say. He stopped. The woman's unnerving stillness was making him wonder if her brother's lunacy ran in the family.

"He was sad," the woman said. "All the time. Ever since he came back from the army. He was empty. I would call him by his name, but it no longer felt like his. But he loved the trains, especially the Celestial Empire."

Hearing the woman say the train's name out loud made Ai Ouyang murmur, "Honorable Lady, speaking of — "

The woman ignored him. "He would walk to the tracks and watch the trains. Always, he would put on his uniform. We were saving up cash to take a ride. I had almost enough strings of it for both of us. I think, now, if I had maybe just … taken what we had, and given it to him, and told him to…"

The breeze rose again. Ai Ouyang could smell the faint perfume of the white flowers next to the tracks.

"You have a grievance," he said.

The woman blinked.

"Yes," she said.

Ai Ouyang waited several seconds. Then he said, "Well?"

"Hero Ai," the woman said, "I want you to avenge my brother. The Celestial Empire must be killed."

Under the woman's white knuckles, the train tracks shifted once, then twice. The clang of the rails nestling against each other was muted, as if the steel was being pressed down against the earth by her hands. Or by the weight of something much heavier.

The air was charged. Ai Ouyang could feel it rising, lifting the hair on the back of his neck, which had grown damp with sweat.

"Lady," he said. "Please. The railway company will pay you for your brother's death. All you have to do is ask them. I'm sure his life was worth at least — I don't know, fifty silver *liang*. Maybe a hundred. But you can talk to them—"

"I don't want the railway company's money," the woman said. She shut her eyes. "I want justice. I want a life for a life. That's why I sent for you, Hero Ai. You are the Hero of Eight Rat Mountain. You understand—"

"But — a train isn't a *life*!"

Behind Ai Ouyang, down the tracks, the whistle of a steam engine echoed. It dipped in pitch, then rose and billowed through the air, proudly, as if a dragon's breath sustained it. The sound was growing louder.

The woman spoke too quietly for Ai Ouyang to hear.

"Get off the tracks!"

He stood. He wanted to reach for her and pull her out of danger. Only the taboo against men touching women without permission stopped him.

The woman released her grip.

Ai Ouyang cried out with relief.

The woman's hands shot forward — and curled in a grip around Ai Ouyang's boot.

"Take my grievance, Hero Ai," she said. "Avenge my brother's death or I will kill myself. If not this train, the next one. If not today, tomorrow. And if not the Celestial Empire..."

A vision, like a spell, blasted across the inner eye of Ai Ouyang's mind.

The vision was of Shanghai, its streets and rivers glowing orange as if lit by fire. Tendrils of white-hot metal snaked from the city's center and grew, twisting outward toward the city walls and beyond, through the villages, out into the countryside. The lines seared Ai Ouyang's inner eye and nearly blinded him. The tracks were writhing and burning, filling the air with billows of smoke and soot and flames.

Ai Ouyang tried to breathe in the April morning air. His lungs felt as if they had been coated with a thick, black poison.

He roared and lunged down toward the woman. Throwing his arms around her waist, he hauled her to her feet. She was so light that his force lifted her feet off the ground. One of her embroidered purple slippers, a shoe the size of a child's, tumbled from her foot and fell between the rails as Ai Ouyang tossed her over his left shoulder.

He dashed to the stone wall. With one hand and the tips of his toes, he climbed the wall, balancing the woman's body on his shoulder under his curled right arm.

On the top of the wall, Ai Ouyang set the woman down on her feet. She winced and bent slightly, reaching for the U-shaped curve of her bare foot.

"You are a devil!" shouted Ai Ouyang.

"No," said the woman, pointing at the train. "*That* is a devil."

A moment later they were engulfed in smoke as the Celestial Empire rolled past on the tracks below them. The roar of its steam engine filled the sky.

When the smoke cleared, Ai Ouyang was still breathing hard. His mouth tasted of ashes. He wanted to spit on the tracks, but didn't because of the woman.

Now that they were both standing, Ai Ouyang could see that she was as tall as he was. She was looking him in the eye.

"I won't have your blood on my hands," he said. "I'll face the train. I accept your grievance. Are you satisfied?"

The woman raised her hands and clasped them together in a gesture of thanks. When she bowed her head and shoulders toward Ai Ouyang, she was smiling.

First, Ai Ouyang tried steel.

He chose a spot near one of the curves in the Woosung Railway where he could wait for the train without being seen. His sword rested in his right hand. He held a dagger in his left.

Beyond these weapons, Ai Ouyang did not have a plan. He had spent an hour praying in a temple that morning trying to think what the Seven-Clawed Tiger might have advised him to do. The effort gave Ai Ouyang a headache. So did the incense, which also made his throat itch and sent him to the inn down the street in search of a drink.

The last train of the evening left Kangwan at 6 o'clock. It was now nine minutes after 6.

The woman sat atop a stack of wooden crates piled next to the tracks, and watched him. Ai Ouyang had put her up there himself. He knew her tiny feet would stop her from jumping down to run onto the tracks if the idea seized her.

The rails twitched and clanked.

Ai Ouyang sighed. He stepped out onto the line.

The fading light caught the sharpened edge of his sword as he lifted it above his head. His left arm was extended, dagger raised. He faced north toward the oncoming train.

When the Celestial Empire rounded the corner, Ai Ouyang heard the Seven-Clawed Tiger's voice over the puffing steam engine.

Look your enemy in the eye.

Ai Ouyang's fear melted away. The approach of the train, now less than one hundred yards away, had hypnotized him into a state of calm acceptance.

It was honorable to fight steel with steel.

Distantly he felt, rather than heard, the force of the train's whistle and the squeal of the brakes being thrown on the engine. The eye of the engine's light was growing brighter and warmer. He could not pull his eyes away.

It looked as if he would lose the fight.

But, Ai Ouyang thought, it would be an appropriate death for a hero. Death facing an enemy would not bring shame to the woman or to the Seven-Clawed Tiger who had taught him since—

You've seen your enemy. Steel won't defeat it.

Ai Ouyang said aloud, "But, Master…"

This is a creature of fire.

The blade lifted above Ai Ouyang's head faltered.

You're enlightened now. Run!

The force of the Celestial Empire's draft as it roared by knocked Ai Ouyang into a spin when he sprang off the tracks. His blades sang, striking the gravel on the railroad bed and throwing up sparks as he rolled and tumbled. He staggered to his feet before the woman without a shred of grace. Even less of his pride remained.

The woman looked down at him, her head tilted.

Ai Ouyang sheathed his sword and tucked his dagger back into his belt.

"I have another idea," he said.

The following evening, Ai Ouyang stood in the same spot on the tracks.

He had had an argument about it with the woman that afternoon. She had wanted him to return to the spot where her brother was killed. Ai Ouyang did not want that; he preferred the presence of the Seven-Clawed Tiger's ghost to that of her dead brother. He also wished she leave him alone to fight the train rather than watching him. The previous night's defeat had been humiliating enough.

They compromised in the end. Ai Ouyang went back to the curve in the tracks. The woman watched.

This time she stood hidden by the wooden crates. She held a flaming torch. Ai Ouyang held no weapons but a drinking gourd in one hand and his brass watch in the other.

It was twenty-three minutes past six.

The last journey of the day, from Kangwan to Shanghai, was late.

Ai Ouyang felt the breeze on his face at the same time that the torch in the woman's hand flared. The tracks clanked and shuddered.

"Now?" the woman asked.

Ai Ouyang shook his head. He tucked the watch into his surcoat pocket.

The Celestial Empire glided around the curve. Ai Ouyang counted his heartbeats, waiting for the whistle to split the air when he was spotted. He opened the gourd.

"Now?" asked the woman.

"Soon," Ai Ouyang said.

The whistle shrieked.

Ai Ouyang lifted the gourd and poured the clear liquid into his mouth. It splashed over the front of his surcoat.

"Now?" the woman asked.

Ai Ouyang nodded at the same time. He held out his hand. The woman handed him the torch.

Ai Ouyang raised the flame to his lips.

He exhaled.

A spectacular fiery plume leaped from Ai Ouyang's mouth. The plume shot through the darkness in a blinding arc toward the oncoming steam engine. The buildings and walls around the tracks danced in the flash of orange-gold light.

Ai Ouyang's lungs pushed flaming air out toward the Celestial Empire until he nearly fainted.

The train's whistle, followed by its brakes, was the shriek of a living thing. Ai Ouyang listened for the sound of pain. When it drew breath and redoubled its cry, the Celestial Empire's whistle sounded even more alive — and triumphant.

Ai Ouyang stopped to inhale. The plume of fire vanished.

Throwing the torch aside, he grabbed the woman's hand and pulled her behind him as he ran, catlike, up the stack of wooden crates.

From the top of the crates Ai Ouyang and the woman watched the steam engine slide to a halt. Lanterns dipped and flashed in the twilight as the driver and brakeman jumped from the train and searched for the source of the fire. After several minutes, the lanterns climbed back into the engine's cab. The train puffed and wheezed to life. It pulled away, toward Shanghai.

"It was beautiful," the woman said quietly.

Ai Ouyang threw the gourd onto the tracks. The sound of it smashing to pieces was the smallest of consolations.

The hero Ai Ouyang disappeared for six days.

On the seventh day the woman received a message:

I have the answer. Meet me near Shanghai Station before the first train tomorrow.

It had been eight days since Ai Ouyang's last attack on the Celestial Empire. They both knew this would bring luck.

The April sun rose on Hero Ai Ouyang standing in the tracks of the Woosung Railway, on the spot in which another man had been killed.

Ai Ouyang held no weapons, not even a drinking gourd. His arms rested loosely at his sides and his hands were empty.

His skin was a deep reddish-brown, the color and consistency of dried blood. He had slicked his long black hair and his clothes with oil and rubbed them thoroughly with the same bloodlike substance. Against the stain, the pale pink of his fingernails and the whites of his eyes shone.

When the woman arrived and saw him, she gasped. "You've been beaten!" she cried.

Ai Ouyang smiled. His teeth gleamed white. He shook his head.

Ignoring taboo, the woman reached out one finger and touched his sleeve. Powder and oil smudged her finger. When she raised it to her nose, she smelled bitterness mixed with iron.

"Rust?" she asked.

Ai Ouyang nodded. His smile broadened. "I had a dream two nights ago. I stood here on the tracks. In my hands was a weapon like a sword, but much heavier. It burned my fingers like fire when I tried to lift it. I looked down. It was a bucket of water."

At their feet, the steel rails chattered against one another.

The whistle of the Celestial Empire blew long and steady from a distance away.

"Though I couldn't see him, I could hear the voice of my master, the Seven-Clawed Tiger." Ai Ouyang gazed down the tracks. "He said *'only water can defeat this dragon. Water will put out its fire and turn it to rust. Become rust. Let it fill your mind. If you feel fear, let the rust eat it away.'*"

The woman and Ai Ouyang heard brakes screeching as the engine began to slow.

Ai Ouyang extended his arms and raised his hands, palms out, fingers together, as if pushing the train back to Shanghai by himself.

"I lifted the bucket," he said. "It weighed almost nothing. I tipped it. When the water splashed out, everything it touched turned to rust. The tracks. The gravel. Even the grass. Then I knew what I had to do. I raised the bucket over my head and poured. The water was warm, thick, like fresh blood. My fear was gone. I woke like this."

The woman examined the tip of her smudged finger. She opened her mouth to taste it.

"No," Ai Ouyang said sharply. "Don't."

"Will I rust?"

"I don't know."

"What are you going to do when the train comes?"

After a moment Ai Ouyang said, "I'm going to let it stare its own death in the eye."

"Please," the woman said. Her voice was low and frightened. "Hero Ai. Don't. It killed my brother. It's going to kill you too."

The Celestial Empire's whistle pierced the morning air.

The train rocked to a stop about thirty yards from Ai Ouyang. The engine driver, a man with hair the color of egg custard and pink-sunburned skin, cupped his hands and shouted in English. They could not understand a word.

The driver scrambled down to the tracks. He was followed by two more English-speaking men. From the cab a Chinese brakeman looked warily at Ai Ouyang but did not move. Nor did the passengers in the coaches, who were craning heads and necks out of the open windows to better see the disturbance on the tracks.

The men circled Ai Ouyang, shouting in a mixture of English and Shanghainese.

The hero stood without moving or speaking. His eyes were fixed on the Celestial Empire.

Smoke rose from her smokestack as she stood, like a dragon chained, breathing steam. If she had been alive, the Celestial Empire would have raked the ground with her claws and writhed with fury.

Historical Note: On August 3, 1876 in Shanghai, a man dressed as a soldier stepped in front of an oncoming steam train and was killed. The suicide ignited a political firestorm between Chinese authorities and diplomats from Britain. The train, called the Celestial Empire, was one of two engines on the first rail line built in China. The line was called the Woosung Railway and had been constructed by a British engineering firm to forge a commercial link under foreign control between central Shanghai and the Yangtze River.

After the suicide, the *taotai* of Shanghai warned the public against riding the Celestial Empire and predicted that hundreds of men might follow the soldier's example. The warning only increased public interest in the "fire dragon carriages."

In October 1877 the Chinese government bought the Woosung Railway from the British and shut down operations within 24 hours.

The tracks were torn up and sold, along with the engines, to Formosa (now Taiwan) for use in a salt mine. For reasons unknown, the railway was never delivered to the mine, but dumped on a beach and left to rust, staining the water and sand the color of dried blood.

Twenty years passed before another steam train ran in Shanghai.

Julia A. Rosenthal is a freelance writer and researcher in Chicago. Her fiction has appeared in *Kaleidotrope* and *A Cappella Zoo* and is forthcoming in an anthology from India-based Zubaan Books. She is working on a novel about the unsolved murder of King Edward the Martyr of England.

Riding the Wind

William H. Keith

"Hey, Coolie! Yer wanted down in the bridge!"

That hated nickname again. Sergeant John Coolidge sighed, handed his wrench to Li Kai, and made his way across the steel deck gratings between the towering masses of engine room machinery. Sergeant Boggs waited for him, hands on hips, face glowering.

"Move it, Coolie. Get your lazy, monkey-lovin' arse in gear!"

"Yes, Staff Sergeant."

What could they possibly want with him in the bridge?

At twenty-eight years of age, Coolidge was the oldest sergeant on board the airship *Victoria Regina*, with little chance for further promotion. He was American, after all, a colonial. Worse, however, both the British Army and the Imperial Airship Service frowned on any officer showing familiarity with the locals. Coolidge had lived in Hong Kong for six years, had learned to speak both Mandarin and Cantonese, and even studied *guo shu* ... something the British Imperial authority always found suspicious, even sinister.

He'd done it to increase his understanding of just what it was the British Empire faced in China. What he appeared to have achieved, however, was the complete stagnation of his military career.

He followed Boggs down a long and narrow passageway. At the end, steel steps led down into the bridge, though members of the Black Gang aft more usually referred to it as "the pit." The Imperial Airship *Victoria Regina* was a full 912 feet long, with two main gondolas suspended beneath her immense envelope. The bridge was located within a secondary gondola at the airship's chin, beneath the forward main gondola. The bulkheads were lined with large windows, slanted to allow the bridge crew to look both out and down at the landscape passing below. As he emerged from the ladder compartment behind Boggs, Coolidge blinked at the sudden explosion of light through those windows. *Victoria Regina* was cruising high above the forested ruggedness of the Dabie Mountains of central China, north of Wuhan.

Colonel Albert Sutherland looked up from one of the bridge telescopes as he entered. "Ah, Staff Sergeant."

"Sah!" Boggs snapped, coming to rigid attention. The staff sergeant had served in the Raj, and his crisp execution of protocol showed it. "I have the individual you requested, Sah!"

"Very good, Staff Sergeant." Sutherland eyed Coolidge. "You're Coolidge?"

"Sir! Yes, sir!"

"The Staff Sergeant tells me you know something of the wogs and their ways. Have a look, here, and tell me if this is something of theirs."

"Sir! Yes, sir!" Coolidge replied with sharp precision, but he wondered what the Colonel could be talking about. The telescope appeared to be trained aft on the airship's keel ... a long and narrow length of structural steel stretching from the bridge all the way aft to the lower stabilizer fin at the tail end of the immense vessel. Accessible from just behind the bridge and by ladder from both main gondolas, the keel possessed wire-rope handrails so that crew members could use it during landing evolutions. Structurally, of course, just as for a sea-going vessel, the keel helped hold the airship's main structure rigid.

The keel was supposed to be kept clear at all times, but there was something there, halfway aft and blocking the walkway. Peering into the eyepiece of the small, gimbals-mounted telescope, he tried to bring it into focus.

A crate was lashed to the keel, its side marked with ideographs. A smaller metal box rested on top, with wires connecting the two.

"What's that woggish writing say?" Sutherland demanded.

"The word on the side of the crate just reads 'Canton,' Colonel," he said. "That smaller device ... I'm not sure, but if I had to guess I'd say it's one of those new *Sakizou* dry cells ... a kind of electrical battery."

"I feared that was the case," Sutherland said, scowling. "Damn and blast! An ID."

"An Infernal Device, yes, sir. There will be a timer of some sort inside the larger box, which probably contains explosives."

"We have saboteurs on this vessel. Mr. Markham! Sound general quarters!"

"Yes, sir," a lieutenant nearby said.

"Staff Sergeant! We need to get rid of that ... device before it damages the ship. I need a volunteer."

"Coolidge!" Boggs rasped. "You just volunteered."

"None of that, Staff Sergeant," Sutherland said sharply. Behind him, an electric bell rasped out the alarm. "This is for volunteers only."

Coolidge licked his lips. The prospect of going out on that narrow walkway to disarm a saboteur's bomb was not a pleasant one.

On the other hand, neither was it pleasant to imagine what would happen if that device exploded before someone else could get out there and disarm it.

"I'll go, sir," he said.

"Eh? Good man. The assassins may be watching it. Markham!"

"Sir!"

"Issue this man a side arm and a knife."

"Sir!"

"We'll be watching from here, Mr. Coolidge," Sutherland told him. "We will have marksmen here to cover you."

Coolidge gauged the distance to the bomb by eye. "That's a good two hundred yards, sir. I hope your men are very good shots."

"None of your lip, Coolie," Boggs said. "Just get out there, cut those lashings, and heave that thing over the side!"

Minutes later, Coolidge stepped out into the thin, cold wind, feeling the grating beneath his feet tremble with the pound of the airship's mighty Daimler engines. The *Victoria Regina* was currently at an altitude of 7,000 feet, high enough that the air bit with each breath despite the fact that it was August. Below, green and torturous mountains reached for the great airship's keel; some of those mountains rose, he knew, to over two thousand feet.

But it still was a long way to fall.

As he stepped out of the shelter afforded by the rear of the bridge housing, the wind caught him from behind, snatching at his hair and clothing. The *Victoria Regina* was cruising at her top speed of approximately forty miles per hour. Her enormous propellers on their masts extending to port and starboard roared as they drove the ship forward and added to the swirling wind. Gripping the cables to right and left, he continued his long walk aft. The steel keel seemed to stretch on and on forever, but at last he was almost there....

Ahead, well beyond the bomb, he saw a figure step down from the aft ladder and begin moving toward him from the airship's stern.

He couldn't tell details at that distance, but the figure wasn't likely to be a friend. It looked like one of the Black Gang coolies. After a moment's hesitation, Coolidge sheathed the knife and reached for his side arm, a heavy .445 Webley revolver. He turned to look back, wondering if Sutherland's marksmen were in place yet ... and only narrowly dodged the sword sweeping toward him.

The sword, a peasant *ni wei dao*, sliced through the starboard-side rope railing and Coolidge's attacker was momentarily off-balance. Where the hell had he come from? Coolidge lunged forward, slamming into the smaller man, pinning his sword arm against the other railing. The man, Coolidge now saw, was Ma Bin, one of the Black Gang coolies, and evidently a Boxer as well.

Coolidge tried to raise his pistol, but Ma fired off a snap kick that caught Coolidge's wrist and sent the heavy Webley spinning out over the railing and into the empty sky below. With his sword arm now free, Ma lunged.

In response, Coolidge twisted and snapped a roundhouse kick that slammed into Ma Bin's chest, knocking him to the side. Coolidge kicked again, higher this time, and Ma pinwheeled wildly for a second, losing his sword, then losing his balance as he gabbed for the rope railing he'd cut just moments before ... and missed. With a shrill wail he went over, falling through the gap in the railing and hurtling into emptiness.

A second coolie advanced behind the first. They'd come down onto the keel, Coolidge now saw, by way of the ladder from the forward gondola. Coolidge dropped into the *xi shi*, the empty-leg stance, all of his weight on his bent right leg, his left leg forward, lightly — "empty" — resting on the toe, hands extended and in line with his nose and forward knee. The second attacker stopped in mid-rush, eyes widening, as he saw Coolidge's *guo shu* stance and realized had happened to his comrade.

Gong fu. The term translated, roughly, as "achievement through great effort." Coolidge had been studying *gong fu* for five years, now — specifically *lung ch'uan*, the southern dragon style.

His interest had been sparked by the various nationalist movements within the Qing Empire of China — especially the Yi He Quan, the Fists of Righteous Harmony, a secret society better known in the West as the Boxers, a name invented by some of the local missionaries. The Boxers practiced various *wu shu* forms, and, like the Ghost Dancers of the American West, claimed supernatural invulnerability to foreign weapons through diet, chants, *wu shu* training, and belief. Superstitious nonsense, of course. Training, dieting, and chanting hadn't helped Ma Bin learn to fly.

The second man, Coolidge was pretty sure, was a coolie with the ship's steward department, one of the boys who set the officer's mess and cleaned up in the galley. He didn't know his name; with fifty British airship personnel on board *Victoria Regina*, and perhaps thirty local workers — WOGS, or "Workers On Government Service" — it had been impossible to keep track of them all. He didn't have a sword like Ma, but as he saw Coolidge's stance, he dropped into a stance of his own — *gong jian shi*, the bow-and-arrow, right leg far out in front and bent, left leg almost straight with perhaps a third of his weight on the ball of the foot.

And the other man, the first one Coolidge had glimpsed, would be coming up now behind him. Coolidge didn't dare turn to look, but he could feel the vibration of the man's feet as he pounded along the keel.

Damn it, where were Sutherland's marksmen? They must be watching from the bridge, must see what was happening.

Don't wait for them to help, he told himself. Find what you need within....

There were two basic approaches to *guo shu*. Where some schools stressed the need for exercise and conditioning, for sheer physical power in strikes and blocks, with an emphasis on the outer form, Dragon *gong fu* and some others stressed instead an inward approach ... developing and raising the *qi* life force that coursed through the world. It was a difference most westerners didn't yet acknowledge, much less understand.

Coolidge drew in a deep breath, then let it hiss sharply on the exhale, a technique for channeling *qi*. Moving with the flow of energy, he crouched and twisted, lashing out with a kick against the steward as he spun to face the attacker behind. The first man shifted, avoiding the blow. Coolidge's left hand snapped out, almost connecting with the second man's throat. Blocked. He kicked, then spun again.

During Coolidge's early training, *Sifu* Hsu, his master in Kowloon, had stressed that one man was superior to two in any fight, because the one fought with a single mind, undivided. Unless these two were very good, their attack would be less than perfectly coordinated. The steward launched a roundhouse kick, his foot sweeping around inches above the railing. Coolidge blocked it with his forearm and snap kicked in return. His riposte was blocked as well, but Coolidge sensed the man was slightly off balance. He kicked again, this time aiming for a kneecap, and felt the crunch, heard the shriek as the blow connected. Twisting back again, he met the other man's attack with clawed hands, twisting aside to avoid the hard-thrust heel of a hand.

He recognized this one as well — Zhu Li, the chief coolie in the aft engine room's Black Gang. Coolidge always had trouble guessing the age of the locals, but Zhu was older than most of the locals on board. That alone gave Coolidge pause; his *sifu* had been in his seventies, and Coolidge had never seen him beaten, not ever.

Dragon stressed fluidity of form and motion, a concept called "riding the wind" which meant following your opponent's movements rather than trying to anticipate them. The emphasis was on turning upper or lower torso without changing stance and on avoiding the opponent's attacks, using sinuous, reptilian movements while breathing to channel *qi*.

His opponent, he saw, was fighting Crane style, a form that also used evasion as a tactic, but which stressed frequent hops and jumps to change stance.

And in that moment, Coolidge knew that he had the clear advantage.

He didn't think it through consciously. He simply reacted — riding the wind. He didn't watch Zhu's eyes, which could be deceptive, but kept his gaze loosely focused on the triangle at the bottom of Zhu's throat, allowing him to see any movement of the man's body almost before it happened.

Zhu hopped, a sudden and elegant shift of stance ... but the narrowness of the keel hindered him, constrained his movement as the attack unfolded into a crane's beak — thumb and forefinger tightly pressed together, arm hooked, hand darting forward toward Coolidge's eye. Coolidge shifted back, avoiding the strike by dropping into *pu tui shi,* the low-leg stretching stance, blocking the crane-strike with the up-sweep of his right hand.

Maybe the advantage wasn't there after all. Stand-off. Both Crane and Dragon preferred to evade, waiting for the opponent to strike and in so doing opening himself to a single, crippling counter-strike.

"Give it up, Zhu," Coolidge said, shouting to make himself heard above the thunder of the engines to left and right. "Your ancestors can't help you here!" It was a deliberate goad. The surname Zhu suggested descent from the Ming emperors, a fact which Zhu used to his advantage when bullying his coolie work force.

"*Gwailo!*" Zhu snapped back, a nasty epithet literally meaning "ghost man," but usually translated as "foreign devil." He hopped forward, changing stance...

...and Coolidge struck, coming up from below, brushing Zhu's kick aside with his right hand, while striking hard at his groin with his left. Zhu fell against the rope handrail, grabbing at it to keep from falling. Coolidge moved up behind him, sweeping Zhu's feet out from underneath him and levering him to the keel's deck.

And then British soldiers were there, coming up from behind with a clatter of boots and rifles. "We got the bloody wog now, Sar'nt," one said. "Nicely done!"

"Damn it, why didn't you shoot?"

"'Cuz you was in the way, Sar'nt!"

It was the work of a moment to slash the lashings of the presumed bomb and tip the crate over the side.

Twelve hours later, the *Victoria Regina* reached Peiping.

The newspapers had been calling it the Boxer Rebellion, a revolt by peasant farmers against both foreigners and the Qing government ... though rumors continued to insist that the Dowager Empress Tzu Hsi herself was behind the uprising. Fifty-five days before, a motley collection of foreign diplomats, Christian missionaries, businessmen, and soldiers from seven different countries had been trapped inside the capital's legation compound by thousands of Boxers. It was said that the attack had been precipitated by a German minister's inexplicable execution of a captured Chinese boy. World opinion, however, was solidly aligned against the Chinese, who were seen as mobs of fanatics and barbarians massacring foreign missionaries and their families and burning the homes of native Christians.

Whatever the rights and wrongs of the uprising, an international force had been dispatched from Tianjin seventy-five miles away, but progress had been slow. The British turreted land cruiser *Behemoth*, it later was learned, had been disabled by a Boxer infernal device exploded against its tracks, and the relief column had stalled.

And so *Victoria Regina* arrived above the capital just after dawn, circling low over the legation compound as the crowd penned inside waved and cheered. Boxer hordes swarmed through the streets beyond the compound walls, a last, surging push to break past the ragged line of defenders before the airship could engage....

Coolidge watched from the forward gondola's viewing gallery as the airship's Maxim guns were turned on the mobs. Most of the Boxers were armed with swords or *guan dao* spears with long, curving tips; the few antiquated rifles among them had no effect on the looming, sun-illuminated splendor of the massive airship above.

Just sixteen years before, a fellow American colonial, Hiram Maxim, had first demonstrated the deadly weapon that now bore his name, and since then it had become the symbol of Imperial colonial might. As Hilaire Belloc had so eloquently put it in "The Modern Traveller":

Whatever happens, we have got
The Maxim gun, and they have not.

Twelve of the weapons firing down through ports in the forward gondola's sides effected a spectacular slaughter, and sent the bloodied survivors streaming back through the city's narrow streets in utter disarray.

The newspapers called it a stupendous victory, a military triumph on the order of Waterloo ... or of New York.

Afterward had come the retribution. Looters ravaged the countryside in so-called punitive raids, killing, raping, burning, and stealing in an orgy of vindictive fury. In addition, China would pay almost a billion *liang* of silver over the next thirty-nine years. Church property would be restored or paid for, and the Qing Dynasty would become the governing arm for foreign powers throughout the Middle Kingdom, especially for the British

Empire, which sought to extend its holdings in Hong Kong deep into the ancient country's interior.

China lay broken and bleeding before the foreign thunderbolt.

And where, Coolidge wondered, was the honor?

Within the tradition of Chinese literature there was the figure of the *wu xia* or "martial hero," the heroic warrior-knight who fought injustice, sought to remove oppressors, fought to right wrongs, helped the oppressed ... a kind of Chinese Robin Hood who adhered to the code of *Xia*.

Imagine, his old *sifu* once had told him, if the ancient Buddhist and Hindu writings were correct ... that just as every life was a multitude of lives, played out over and over as the soul matured and advanced, the universe, too, was but one of an infinity of universes, cycles upon cycles of them. In such a multitude of realities, everything and anything would be possible.

Imagine, *Sifu* Hsu had said, universes where the British Imperium never existed ... where the American Rebellion had succeeded or the Raj in India had collapsed, worlds where the fictional Sherlock Homes was real, or the real-life Boxers were fiction. All of those possibilities not only could exist but must exist somewhere within the multiverse, all of those, and so many, many more.

And why, his *sifu* had continued, would this universe of universes continue to play out the dramas of life again and again? Coolidge himself, *Sifu* Hsu had pointed out with that character-istic twinkle in his eye, might have played countless different roles across those infinities of worlds — farmer, banker, lawyer, politician, soldier, pauper, lord ... and why?

Might it be to allow him, his soul, to learn how to live, no matter what the external circumstances of that life?

In life, as in *gong fu lung ch'uan*, the student had to learn to ride the wind....

And perhaps a part of that was to learn how to live as a *wu xia*, with honor, giving justice, helping the downtrodden, in a universe that seemed not to care about such insubstantial niceties.

Coolie. Monkey-lover. A soldier of the Empire gone native....

John Calvin Coolidge, Jr. — born on July 4th, 1872 in the tiny village of Plymouth Notch in the Republic of Vermont, a lowly sergeant in the British Imperial Airship Service who happened to believe that the Chinese were people, were humans deserving of respect — drew himself up to his full five-foot ten.

Perhaps, just perhaps, in this universe a *wu xia* could make a difference....

William H. Keith is author of over 100 books, including three New York Times bestsellers. His pseudonyms include H. Jay Riker (military fiction) and Ian Douglas (military SF). This is his first foray into the Steampunk genre. A former Navy hospital corpsman, he lives in the mountains of western PA.

Mistress of the Pearl Dragon

Shen Braun

Topper had just watched the bloody dragon eat three bloody Chinamen, so he had no patience for beggars. He stalked through the dirt streets of the godforsaken Chinese village, well-practiced at avoiding the silently pleading wretches and townsfolk both. All he wanted was to get back to his ship, tap into a keg, and calculate how much the bloody Mistress was going to cost him this time, but a persistent sod blocked his way.

"Englishman," the beggar said. "Stop and I will pay you for your time." He jingled his sleeve. Topper knew that sound well enough, but it was the perfect English from the Chinese mouth that stopped him.

"New to this begging thing, I see," Topper said. He gave the fellow a sardonic once-over. Shorter than Topper but tall for a Chinaman, his tunic and trousers were black silk and his hair was pulled back into a braid that dropped nearly to his waist. He certainly didn't match the street's ragged chaff.

"I am buying, not begging," the man said. "That is your custom, yes?"

It was, but the bald statement made Topper uncomfortable. "What do you want? I'm a busy man." He pulled out a hip flask and took a pinch.

"My name is Kuo Kun Tien. With your help, I will challenge the Pearl Dragon."

Topper choked on the whiskey. He coughed, thumping his chest. The Chinaman stood impassive. Finally Topper said, "You're mad, mate, completely nutters. No one goes in there."

"You have. Twice. And both times, you have come out free and unharmed."

"The dragon only eats at the order of its Mistress, you see, and I have what she craves. Simple as that."

"Opium." The word was flat, but Topper heard an undertone.

Topper sampled his flask again. "If it weren't me, it'd be someone else, mate. Way of the world."

For a moment Topper thought the Chinaman was going to swing at him. It'd be the last thing the fool ever did, but if he wanted to see the dragon, his end was coming anyway.

Instead, Kuo only said, "Will you do it?"

"You don't need me to hold your hand if you want to get chewed up," Topper said. He gestured toward the compound he'd just left. "The dragon takes all comers."

"I am not allowed inside. The Mistress of the Dragon has forbidden it."

"Why's that?"

"I have sworn to destroy her."

That wiped the smirk off Topper's face.

They found a place that served something harder than tea. Topper said, "No one beats the dragon, mate. I hate dealing with the Mistress, the vicious bint, but my well-wishes won't mean much when her pet's crunching your bones."

With the money the Mistress made from her opium smuggling, she could have made her village — hell, the whole province — into paradise on earth. Instead, she hoarded it all and kept her people on the brink of starvation. The only way out was to challenge the dragon. Losing meant your death, but at least your suffering was over. Topper had seen the hideous end of so many challengers; the Mistress used them as grisly intimidation to haggle over prices.

"I will not lose," Kuo said. He laid his right hand on the table between them. For the first time Topper noticed it was covered by a thick glove. He knew what that meant. Kuo had one of those new bronze hands — maybe his whole arm — and was keeping it as a surprise to spring on the Mistress. It might even work. Maybe.

"That's a grand piece," Topper said. He peered at the limb. The thing looked completely natural. "Where'd you get it?" He knew plenty of sailors with missing parts who'd be interested. "What's the power source? Can't be steam. Tesla battery?"

"*Qi.*"

Topper rolled his eyes. That again. These Easterners had a lot of weird beliefs. "Fine, don't tell me." He took a sip from his crude ceramic mug; the wine was harsh but warming. "Let's say your plan works. The dragon'll be beaten, you'll have its pearl, but the fifty or so guards the Mistress has will gut you. More importantly, they'll gut me."

"No. She rules by fear that flows from the dragon. Stem that flood and her power vanishes."

That was true. "If I bring you inside, I want the pearl. If you get it, that is."

Kuo sat like a stone.

"Why not, mate?" Topper said. "You hand it over, that'll be one less Englishman selling opium, you can believe that. There's no way I'm still taking ship when I could buy Buckingham Palace. We both win."

Kuo nodded one single jerk of his head.

The compound where the Mistress laired was as fortified as an English castle and it dominated the village center. Its high stone walls were warm to the touch and Topper knew why: inside were engines that cooked day and night. Not only did they heat the entire compound during the cold winter nights but they were set to release a blast of super-heated steam if anyone tripped one of the pressure triggers along the wall's top. The unfortunate thief would be boiled alive. If you didn't have wings, the gates were the only way in.

All the guards knew Topper by sight, and nodded at his approach. Then they recognized Kuo and went for their weapons.

Topper held up his hands. "Easy, boys, easy. This one's a gift for the Mistress." He grinned, all amiable. "He wants to challenge the dragon. From what I hear, she'd be happy to let him try." He tipped the guards a wink to show them what he thought of Kuo's chances.

The guards laughed. They knew just what challenging the dragon involved: it was a death sentence. "We search you."

They were perfunctory with Topper, just part of the routine, but patted the stoic Kuo down thoroughly. Topper was worried they'd notice the metal of the Chinaman's arm, even when swathed under layers of fabric, but they never balked. Eventually satisfied there was nothing dangerous on them — ha! fools! — the guards threw the heavy locks and opened the gate.

They were marched to the central keep, a squat three stories of cut stone. A guard pushed open a massive bronze door and gestured: Topper and Kuo were to go in by themselves to face the Dragon's Mistress.

One step inside and Topper almost tripped over his own feet. It was the dragon, of course, the great Pearl Dragon. He'd seen the bloody thing a hundred times and it still scared him senseless.

It was a serpent thicker through the middle than a tall man, and its horrible bronze-scaled length was heaped around the room in ever-writhing coils. Twin rows of gleaming spikes marched up its lean reptilian head. Golden eyes, big as cannon shot, glared out from under iron brows. It lifted its head at their entrance. Hot steam drifted from its nostrils.

"You bring my enemy here?" the Mistress shrieked. The dragon snarled.

Bloody hell.

Topper swallowed. Two grim-faced guards flanked the Mistress, pistols in hand, ready to kill at her command. Servants kept her cool with fans while others hovered near to tend to her whim. Her age was impossible to know, but the Pearl Dragon's Mistress was slender and strikingly beautiful, even in anger. Nails and lids and lips were painted blood red, and she always wore scarlet silk robes of the highest quality. She hadn't stood from the lounging couch where she lay and hadn't discarded the stem of her opium pipe. Maybe she wasn't as mad as all that.

"I did," he said, "and you can thank me for it later." Boldness was his best bet. "He's unarmed, alone, and here to challenge the dragon."

For a moment he worried while she continued to glare, but then her sensual lips curved into a wolf's smile. "Is this true?" she asked Kuo.

"It is."

She clapped in delight, suddenly young as a child. "Come forward, then." Turning to the dragon she purred, "Someone wishes to test you, my love."

The head slid forward and rose. Its jaws opened, revealing row upon row of curved, razor-sharp fangs. Topper heard the faint hiss of hidden pistons at work. Wider and wider the maw grew until there was more than enough space for any idiot to waltz right in. Slowly, the pearl was revealed.

At the back of the dragon's throat it hung, suspended between two naked electrical contacts. It was bigger than Topper's fist. The gorgeous thing was amplifier and regulator both, channeling the power that drove the dragon. Without it, the machine would die.

A solid shield of glass blocked access to the pearl. It was the same kind of stuff they'd used in the latest bathysphere; nothing less than a cannon was going to punch through. To get your hands on the pearl, you had to step inside the dragon's terrible jaws, then snake your arm down and around the shield, with the articulation gears at the back of the throat ready to rip through your flesh. Speed was impossible. There would be no quick snatch and grab. Fail and the jaws closed. Hard.

Kuo didn't hesitate. He strode forward without fear.

"Stand with me, Topper," the Mistress said. "We shall have a fine view of his end."

He did as she ordered, unable to stop watching Kuo. "Crazy buggar," he muttered.

"I shall enjoy this," the Mistress crooned.

Topper barely heard her. Kuo was at the dragon. It hissed again, bathing him in a cloud of steam. Topper flinched but Kuo ignored the display and entered the jaws.

Deadly fangs surrounded Kuo`s legs and hung around his head. He positioned himself near the glass shield in front of the pearl and lowered his head. Every eye in the room — guard, servant, Topper, Mistress — was riveted.

Kuo struck.

His right arm blurred forward. There was a resounding crack. Before the shards of glass could even begin to fall, Topper saw the pearl was gone. Kuo clutched it to his side.

Chaos exploded in the room. The Mistress screamed. Her two guards raised their pistols. Servants scattered.

Topper stepped forward and slapped both his hands onto the shoulder of the nearest guard. The connection completed, a lightning storm's worth of electricity snapped from the contacts on Topper's palms into the guard. The guard howled; his body galvanized into rigor and he collapsed.

The other guard whirled and Topper found himself staring down the too-wide barrel of a cocked pistol.

"Easy, there," Topper said, backing away, hands up. His little trick was only good for a single jolt, more's the pity, and he had no other weapon. Topper's attempt at a friendly smile felt greasy and unconvincing.

The guard's trigger finger tightened. Topper winced, seeing his life about to end in a roar of gunpowder when Kuo appeared from nowhere.

One hand knocked the gun aside. It went off with a deafening boom. The round careened harmlessly off the floor. Kuo's other hand, the right one, the deadly one, drove into the guard's neck. The man dropped.

Silence had fallen. The servants had all fled. Behind Kuo, Topper could see the dragon lying motionless, dead, flat across the floor.

The Mistress was sprawled on her couch, red eyes closed. Topper thought she was dead, too, then saw her chest rise and fall. She'd only fainted. He grinned.

"Thought she was made of sterner stuff than that," Topper said.

Kuo regarded her without mercy. "I was not fooled."

"Good for you, mate." He caught a flash of movement. Someone peeked into the room through the main door, then darted away. A guard, Topper was sure of it, and he'd seen the fear and relief plain on the man's face before it'd vanished. "I think you were right about their loyalty," he said. "She's finished." When Kuo said nothing, Topper gave him a pointed look. That got him nowhere, either. He whistled softly between his teeth. Subtlety was lost on this one but he could do blunt if that's what was needed.

"Well, you got what you wanted," Topper said. "Now it's time for me to get what I want." He held out a hand. "Give it up, mate."

Wordless, Kuo extended his right hand to Topper. It still gripped the pearl. Bloody hell, he'd hit the guard with the pearl! Topper peered at it in panic, hoping it wasn't cracked. He breathed a sigh of relief; it looked fine.

Then he looked again. There were streaks of blood on the prize. The black glove had great rents in it, made when Kuo had punched through the unbreakable glass. Through them Topper could see bleeding and ripped flesh. Kuo's hand wasn't bronze or iron or anything other than human skin and bone.

He stared at Kuo, dumb-struck.

A faint hint of a smile teased at Kuo's mouth. "I did not lie: powered by *qi*."

Bloody hell.

Shen Braun is a dedicated writer, parent, nerd, house-husband, and gamer (not necessarily listed in order of importance). The product of a childhood spent reading and role-playing, it's only natural he prefers to write stories that just can't happen in the real world.

Song of My Heart

Jennifer Rahn

When Jianyu was born, he was a great disappointment to everyone. Heads hung in shame, the elders bore the intensity of Grandfather's glare, made more fearsome by the old man's white hair tossing over his black robe as he moved. Jianyu, the fat thief of *Qi*, squirmed in his cradle, unaware of how badly he had damaged the Sphere of Wu Shin. Although the brass plates remained solid and the rivets held strong, our enclosed City was fragile, barely maintaining its balance with the other floating City-Spheres of the Lake. Not only had Jianyu's birth increased the presence of Yang, he had also completely wiped out any compensating effect of his mother's Yin, having killed her with his arrival.

Distant shouts could now be heard as men scurried to find any fuel for the burning maws of the steam-driven equilibrium-engines that fought against the disparity. The floor shuddered intermittently, and the balancing pumps shrieked with strain, trying to maintain Wu Shin's steadiness. The positioning of Grandfather's City-Sphere within the Taijitu Spiral was supposed to be in perfect harmony with the other Spheres, creating the music of enlightenment. It hardly sounded that way now.

Unable to control his fury any longer, Grandfather smashed the jade emblem of Jianyu's birth against the wall. He stormed out, followed immediately by the uncles and father of this unwanted, impetuous disaster. The baby could not notice the shift of our Sphere closer to the outer rim of the Spiral, so he continued to kick and wave his fat feet and hands in the presence of his only aunt, Lihua.

Lihua was a lady of great composure. Her fan and the red dust around her eyes may have hidden any upset, yet this time she could not prevent her tears from spilling into rivulets of black that ran down the powdered white of her face. Releasing a deep sigh, she finally shifted in the heavy red and cream silks that encased her, the rustling of her sleeves and blossom-adorned hair alerting her servants that she wished to leave. They helped her rise, leading her gently over the red and gold carpet, her footsteps leaving brief impressions of heat that glowed in my ocular input.

I, too, could now leave the chamber; yet temptation stirred in my little gyrating pumps that mimicked a heart. Pistons and valves quivered, clearly visible though the silica encasing my inner works — I was low on *Qi*, the midnight blue force pumping through my veins gradually fading each day to silver. My knee gears caught and ground as I went to the crib to gaze at the small organic creature with great jealousy. He stopped his squirming to look through the skin above my lilac dress, mesmerized by the churning pumps and gears he could see within my throat. They made soft squeaking noises, now that they were old and misaligned.

So much *Qi*. His body pulsated with the glowing, vital energy, all gotten so easily by simply being organic. A few drops of it would have energized me for years — but it was forbidden. Such things could only be given by the elders, and only when it was not needed for the great stabilizing engines. I turned and exited the room slowly so that I would not stumble and fall, losing my wig, and smashing myself yet again. The exorbitant cost of parts and labour had caused my husband to do many of the repairs himself. The disfigurement was … well, Fuhua was a good man. Certainly he appreciated my efforts to compensate.

At the docks, I stood beside Fuhua as he gazed past the wooden planks, into the resplendent orange glow reaching over the water surrounding the Sphere. He watched longingly as Lihua's golden junk lifted its sails and ran its pumps until it released a huge plume of steam, carrying her back to the safety of the Spheres that were better balanced and closer to the Centre of the Spiral. One of her status — female and organic — was free to live where she wished. A woman such as her would most certainly not stay here. Our Sphere was already too far away from the centre of the Spiral and there would be little she could do to rescue it.

"Song." Grandfather turned to me as he said my name. I bowed as humbly as I could without overstressing my gyros and tipping over. "You will look after the child when we are not using him."

Using? I bowed again, not daring to question my elder. Grandfather regarded me longer, as if considering how much explanation he would provide.

"One generation more and we will be pushed out entirely, free-floating in the Lake, completely dependent on our own means. There will be no more women here, and thus no new *Qi*. Jianyu has cost us dearly. He will repay his debt to our Sphere. Our energy must come from somewhere." I bowed once more, still not understanding, but honoured by Grandfather's trust. I reached for Fuhua's hand, as he must also have been pleased by this, but he had already left. How foolish of me. How unreasonable to expect that my existence could satisfy his longing when a real woman had just been here.

I stood motionless for perhaps an hour. My memory capacitors had grown faulty, and I was experiencing lapses of consciousness. By the time I regained awareness, the dock was cleared. Only the piercing cries of Jianyu could be heard back within the Sphere. It took me a while longer to move toward him, not because I was frozen, but because…

Fuhua had not returned for me. Before he always had.

I finally reached the cradle, and stared down at the squalling organic, confused. Being an organic had always elevated a person, even one so unwanted, and yet here he was, as abandoned as I. It had to be something else, then, that determined the importance of a person. I collected him from the cradle, hugging him to my breast as I had seen real women do in holograms. This did nothing to comfort the child, yet it amazed me when the pulsating life forces in his body radiated through my silica casing. He was soft, warm and yielding, squirming against me. It felt nothing like the presence of my husband, when he used to come to my bed. Jianyu's energies were unconstrained, and shared freely. I aligned my Kirlian plates towards him to receive what I could. Surely I could collect a little of this energy that he dispersed anyway?

I took the baby to my chambers where a small brass tank with many levers and gears stood upon three sturdy legs. After turning the small crank at the front once, I held the feeding tube extending from the base of the tank to Jianyu's mouth, letting him suckle until he fell asleep. I sat there, thinking that Fuhua would return, see me in my finest silks holding this child, and desire me as he had when I was first constructed.

Time passed and Jianyu grew. Because we were alone, I spoke to him, feeling ever so pleased when he eventually spoke back. We continued on in this way — feeding and conversing — for many years. I watched his hair and beard grow long and thick as he became a man, his body fill out and stretch until he could only place his head in my arms when it came time to feed. Fuhua never returned. Perhaps he had died.

The elders came to take Jianyu away for a few hours each week. He always shied away from them when the door opened and the radiated light of their bodies fell into the room. Sometimes he would scurry under my heavy, mahogany table and fight them, kicking and punching furiously. They would grab his clothes to pull him out, and when those had been torn away, they would grab his hair and skin, forcing him to leave, dragging the energy of his *Qi* out of my chambers. Whenever Jianyu was gone, my world was dark.

I sat alone yet again, waiting for my door to swing open and his body to be dumped through its frame. Despite the easing of my being that occurred whenever he was returned to me, the current in my body always fluctuated drastically when he told me what they had done to him.

"They drain me, Song. Trap me in a cage so I can't move, push metal probes through my skin and sap my life to power their machines."

I cradled him in my arms and comforted him as best I could, holding the feeding tube to his lips and searching my databases for stories that would distract him from his pain and soothe him into sleep. Over several days, the light of his *Qi* regenerated — until the elders returned.

And again. I sat alone in my chamber, surrounded by so many beautiful items — sculpted jade, wooden screens, silk draperies, empty silica of others like me who no longer held a charge — all these lovely things that no one seemed to value without the energy of life.

When my door opened at last, Jianyu's body was so dark that I thought they had drained him completely. He flopped from their hands onto my carpet. My heart pumps stuck for a moment, but a faint flicker of energy still lingered around his heart and lips, barely detectable by my ocular input.

"Jianyu," I whispered, shifting my weight and grinding my knee gears to reach him. I needed him. Neither Grandfather nor Fuhua had given me even a single drop of *Qi* for years. All that kept me going was the small amount I collected with my Kirlian plates.

Moving carefully, I lifted and carried him back to my couch, then raised the feeding tube to his mouth. A single drop of glistening white fell from its end, then nothing more. Our resources were cut off. I had nothing to give him except...

My brass sewing shears, which lay in a basket by my feet, more for decoration than use, did have sharpened edges. I poked a hole in the silica of my chest, awkwardly working the blades in a circle until the opening was big enough to insert my fingers. I reached in to where my little whirring pumps were connected to the series of tubes through which my *Qi* flowed, and pulled one free. A silver-blue drop fell from its end as I held it over Jianyu's mouth, but it puddled listlessly around his tongue. He was unable to use the *Qi* in this form. I could use it because...? My memory slipped for a moment.

Because Grandfather had used his alchemy to mould extracted *Qi* into *jin*, which could power the elemental metals, but could not be returned to an organic. Jianyu! Was there nothing else I could give him? Reaching into my chest again, I deliberately ground my thoracic gear over my hand, releasing a fine spray of metal. I put this into Jianyu's mouth, wiping my fingers against his lips. His hungry blood swept it away and his light seemed to shift toward infrared.

Slowly, his system accepted the energy as it dripped from the tube in my chest, glowing with the same metallic blue that ran in my veins. The sensation of the *Qi* transfer was amazing. I could feel synchronicity between his heart and my pumps as both beat to the rhythm generated by my *jin*. Was this how it felt to be organic and alive?

Every bit of *jin* exited my body and filled Jianyu, carrying more of my metal components as it left. I happily surrendered, as this was my will. I went blind as my systems sequentially failed, but in the seconds before I lost my sight I saw the Sphere through his eyes, now enhanced with my ocular input. So beautiful! I could see his cells meld and mutate to become more than merely organic or mechanical. A whole greater than the parts.

Tendons and muscles found simpler, purer forms while his intellect rewired itself. Before I finally lost my sense of touch, I was able to feel his pleasure at the enhanced sensation of running his fingers over the silks covering my arm, and at his new mechanical receptors feeding him information about the exact positioning of each fingertip as he flexed his hands with their metal wires snaking through them. Before my neural network completely faded, I felt him turn to look at me and marvel at what an amazing creation I was. How strange. Fuhua had never thought so.

And then, my consciousness ended.

Restart.

I am ... Jianyu. I am...

I didn't know what I was. But I knew I was beautiful. Perfection. My form was dark, long and sleek; elegant with curves of metal and muscle now fused into a hybrid of organic and machine. Between stretches of translucent flesh, tendons and endoskeleton were interspersed with arteries and tubes carrying *jin*. Within my chest, the motion of tiny mechanical metal pumps assisted my circulation, creating a system stronger than before. At my feet lay the remains of what had been Song, just a mound of deflated silica.

Song. Still in my heart. My strength flared with her essence but she had never been real Yin and I was no longer Yang. I had strange, new sort of balance. I flexed my will and felt the Sphere of Wu Shin spin even farther from the edge of the Spiral. I could hear Grandfather and the elders scream and run for the central stabilizers. Their panic no longer distressed me. I could change things.

I could be anything, exist in any circumstance, absorbing new energies from any element that surrounded me. I saw what our Sphere was and what it could be and that I would soon make everything right. My elders would finally have prosperity and peace.

Zichan fuzhai. I balanced myself. My breath drew in. My arms moved in sweeping arcs, my right foot extended in front of me. Poised. Breath expelled out sharply as I pulled my arms back, fists tucked by my sides.

Shen ti xing. I was the vessel ready to be filled. I made a half turn and shifted my weight to my other foot, repositioning my arms in front of my body. The power of the elements came into me from beyond the Sphere. No longer would we be dependent on the Taijitu Spiral.

Li. My strength swirled within me.

Yi. I released this energy into Wu Shin, to power my family's home, letting them know I could sustain us all. My arms opened and swept down as the *Qi* came out from me in waves.

Jing. I released all my love, the Song in my heart, into the structure of Wu Shin. Our Sphere stopped its motion. The entire structure, every atom, was in a state of flow, of perfect balance within the Lake.

The elders broke down the door. I searched their faces eagerly for Fuhua, whom I did not find. Grandfather came forward, his eyes flashing as he pounded the heel of his staff once, and all fell silent.

He did not yet understand.

I smiled, wanting to share my new knowledge. "Grandfather, I have made things stable. We no longer need the Taijitu Spiral. We are a new centre of balance, all by ourselves."

"Jianyu?" He glared at me, his eyes raking across my changed body with what looked like disgust. "What has that abomination done to you? I will restore you at once!"

"Abomination? Grandfather, no! Let me show you—"

"You have lost your humanity! And you will not show anyone anything!"

My elders shifted behind Grandfather and I saw they were armed. Again I had been foolish. All his talk of balance, the maintenance of order. Grandfather only wanted power that he alone could control and provide. The rage on his face told me all.

Grandfather slammed his staff down again, and my elders moved in to attack. *"Zhe shi mogui."*

So be it. *I am a devil indeed.*

"Be still, Jianyu! I will remove that traitorous metal from you!"

They would not take Song from me, returning me to that living death. The elders' blows were sluggish, easy for me to predict and avoid. I was not as they tried to make me believe. They were not as they tried to make themselves believe. Why should I keep trying to please these … archaic … useless…

My heart broke. So long had I yearned for their affection that the wish still resided within me, but my defence was sure, my strikes were precise, brutal.

I could not kill them.

I fled. I ran through the halls of Wu Shin, through the steam-filled underworkings, out into the darkness of the Lake. I swam through the icy waters, not caring that soon I would be lost, and more alone than I had ever been.

And then I heard it, the Music of the Spheres. The part of me that was Song resonated with it. But — it did not come from the Taijitu Spiral. It came from without, somewhere above the waters. I looked up into the sky, never before having thought about what might be beyond the Lake. Could it be that there was more than all this? I had focused on Grandfather and his given Law for so long, that I had never considered...

I lifted my arms, letting my Kirlian aspects absorb *Qi* from all elements of the Universe. It called to me, and I answered a million souls that had escaped this muddy empire for a different kind of life. Empowered, my being lifted into the air, gently spiralling with the balance known to the Taijitu. I was, in myself, everything I needed to be.

It only took a moment, a precise pearl of centred harmony within my being to accept myself and release the false cloak I had worn. I left the Taijitu, taking Song with me and began my journey toward the next existence. The Universe embraced me, caressing me with its varied energies, giving me the promise that I would never again be refused as part of the Whole.

Jennifer Rahn is the author of the novels Wicked Initiations and The Longevity Thesis. She has also published several short stories in various Canadian and American anthologies. Jen currently works in both academia and biotech, where she researches ways to improve the outcome of glioblastoma multiforme.

Last Flight of the Lóng Qishi

Emily Mah

The beggar arrives at sundown, his posture stooped as a shepherd's crook, feet cracked and tough as old leather. His face is so lined with wrinkles that his eyes are nothing more than slits. A wispy gray beard sprouts from his chin and trails to one side in the wind. There is always wind in the city that time has forgotten and tonight it bears the scent of moisture and the promise of a storm.

With its tireless gusts the wind has broken down the old, stone walls, leaving them in ruin, and has scattered gears, parts of old vehicles, machines, and even people along with bits of carapace across the roads now buried in sand. There is a glass eye that stares blankly at the heavens. Across the way is a leg worked in iron, the padded sling atop it all rotted away.

This was a city of survivors, but now it is only a ruin. In its shadows flits a tiny figure, a little slip of a girl, who peers out between the cracked bricks with interest. Who is this old man who's come so far across the wasteland? How did he survive temperatures that bake water right out of the skin by day and freeze one solid at night? What would he seek in a place so forsaken as this?

He seems unaware of her as he makes his way, a catch in his step that is not quite a limp, down the dusty memory of a street towards the far edge of town. His course is straight and implies purpose. Past two turns, the girl begins to guess where he is going; when he bears right at the next, she flies across the broken stones, moving like a darting shadow through the ruins, her gaze always fixed on the old beggar.

Her pulse quickens as he reaches the open area, once a town square, and pauses to look at the great wreckage that spans it like a fallen bridge, all rusted metal ribbing and great swathes of torn fabric, gears that are so gummed with sand that they will never turn again.

None of this gives the beggar pause. He walks to the far end of the wreck, stops, stoops, and pushes aside a handful of sand. One great glassy eye stares back at him, and the girl sees his wrinkles deepen in a smile.

Quick as a bird, the girl darts away to the little shanty town built up inside the old market. Gone are the cloth awnings that covered stalls of sweetmeats and trinkets, replaced by the ragtag shelters that stink of stale smoke and raw sewage. The broken roof, high above, gives some cover from the elements. "A *Lóng Qíshì!*" she cries out across the expanse of cookfires and junkpiles. Patched together automatons rattle in surprise at her shout. "A *Lóng Qíshì!*"

No human looks up. "She is a simple minded girl," people whisper. "A little slip of a fool, nothing more." "The Dragon Riders are a myth!" shouts one man.

But by the time she returns to the square with a dipper full of rainwater, the beggar has moved enough sand to reveal a lion-like face with two great glass eyes that shine without any scratches. A large mouth with white teeth and a curling tongue grin in the setting sun. A light wind dances along the length of the behemoth and vast lengths of cloth stir and billow, casting sand aside.

On the horizon sit dark clouds, gravid with rain, trundling inevitably closer like battle tanks from the Great War. A strong wind, laden with water droplets, snakes across the square, pushing rivers of sand before it, causing the great sails of cloth to lift and furl, ripples cascading along the length of the whole tangled wreck.

The beggar places his hand on one great glass eye and holds still as stone, save for a smile that folds his heavily creased skin again and again. With a sudden laugh, he claps his hands. The girl cups the dipper of water against her chest and braves the wind to go to him. She keeps her head bowed as she presents the water, and the beggar touches it first to his forehead, then his lips, drinking it dry in one draught.

With a grinding creak, gears begin to move in the wreckage beside them. Old gears so gritted with sand that they have been locked for decades now begin to turn, grinding like old bones. Two great wings, ripped and tattered, extend towards the stars. The grinning mouth snaps open then shut and the great glass eyes close with a click and open with a clack.

The girl tears herself away and flies to the marketplace again. "He has awakened the dragon!" she cries. "He has brought it back!"

But not even the automatons look at her now. She is clearly raving. What wild stories she has, first of a *Lóng Qíshì* and now a dragon coming to life in the ruins of the city.

Someone throws a rock and it pelts her in the arm. She startles and moves away. Quickly, before more stones rain down, she runs out into the deepening night and the encroaching storm.

"You see what a fool she is?" the junk dwellers say. "She is touched in the head."

Out in the encroaching darkness, she picks her way back to the square. When the sun goes down, wild dogs begin to stir, hunting across the dunes in their packs.

The girl reaches the beggar just as the whole wreck spins to life. Gears turn flywheels that pivot the great wings to catch the wind, only to have it pour on through the holes and tatters in the cloth. Try as they might to cup the air, they jerk and rattle to no avail. More gears begin to turn and the eyes blaze with light. The jumble of rags and scrap shudders and begins to rise. Out of the grit rises a metal seat, like a throne, and the sand pours off it like water.

The beggar claps again and shouts for joy, only to have his voice drowned out by a crash of thunder. With halting steps he draws near enough to catch the side of the great lion face, and as the wind screams past, the sinuous neck lifts him up to the chair. He grabs one armrest, spry as a young man for a moment caught in the eyeblink of blinding white lighting that strikes out in the desert and imprints his image on the girl's retinas.

As the thunder rolls towards the ruins, coming ever louder, she races back to the old market. "He is leaving!" she cries. "The *Lóng Qíshì* is leaving! He and the dragon will fly!"

She dodges one stone, and then another, but is not quick enough for the woman who grabs her by the arm. "There are no *Lóng Qíshì*," the woman spits, her broken teeth causing her to whistle as she speaks. "They were a myth. They never were. The Great War, the Pulse that killed the automatons, they're stories, girl. Be sensible."

"You'll miss it," the girl says, chin up with grim determination. She ducks under the woman's slap and wriggles free from her grasp. The next flash of lightning shows the girl leaping through the doorway, back out into the night.

"You'll die!" the woman shouts after her, only to have the wind tear her words from her mouth.

The wind is so strong that it almost lifts the girl off her feet, but she runs ever onward towards the square. The dragon's lights flicker and its gears splutter. One wing has been torn to ribbons by sand borne on the gale.

In the lee of a large stone, the girl cowers and peers into the rain drenched darkness. The dragon lights, then stills, then lights again. The beggar sits calmly in his throne, serene, at peace.

The wind screams through the empty walls and broken stones of the city and funnels of sand and rain spin up in the distance. The girl presses herself more firmly in place and strains to see the dragon, now dark, now dim, bright for a heartbeat, then dim again. A broad section of fabric has torn away from the metal frame, but still the beast stirs, still it lifts its snakelike neck with the rider atop.

A gust strong enough to slide stones across the sand heaves the great beast over, then up. The broken wings flap and the long, lean body tumbles up into the air, now flashing bright, now dim, now gone, only to flash black against the white clouds in the next blink of lightning.

Burned into the girl's retinas is the image of the dragon aloft, the rider with his arms outstretched, guiding the beast masterfully through the air, the wings unfurled, and the five-clawed talons poised to strike.

But as the thunder rolls in, shaking the very ground with its wrath, the now bright, now dim, lights tumble away into the darkness, carried up to the heights of the clouds, perhaps, or dashed against the desert below.

The girl strains to see in the pouring rain and howling wind, but each flash of lightning shows only empty sky.

The storm rages on, the night darkening to pitch, like a cavern. More funnels weave across the desert, tossing sand and rocks high into the air.

The wind screams on, until morning, when the first fingers of the dawn reveal a sky scrubbed clean of clouds and devoid of dragons. The girl sits, shivering but alive. She looks down at her hands, marveling that they are still there, still move when she bids them. Her dress is torn up one side, but covers her well enough. The ground beneath her feet is chill and still wet, even as the thirsty earth drinks down the puddles so fast that they appear to boil, and a piece of bright gold cloth is caught on a rough stone nearby.

She gets to her feet and limps to the market again, the image of the last *Lóng Qíshì* branded in her heart, the scrap of brightly colored cloth in one hand.

Let them laugh, she thinks. When the first of the inhabitants calls out to her, "What of your dragon?" she gives no reply. Instead she thinks of the great square, now being combed smooth again by the wind and time until it too remembers no more.

Emily Mah Tippetts writes science fiction and fantasy as Emily Mah and YA romance as E. M. Tippetts. Her father's side of the family immigrated to the United States from China in the 1940's. A former attorney with degrees in philosophy, politics and economics from Oxford University and business law from UCLA, she now lives in London with her family. It's a long way from New Mexico, where she grew up.

Protection from Assassins

Frances Pauli

Leilani only stole a pinch. One tiny press of powder from each packet and the old apothecary would never know.

She crouched in the alley behind the crates and fishermen's nets, her nose scrunched against the smell of Kona's main port, with six perfect, square packets spread on the cobbles like Mahjong tiles.

Her fingers slipped a glass vial from a secret compartment in her lacquer belt. Just a few more trips to market on the apothecary's business and she'd have enough of a stash.

Zing! A thick, bronze bolt smashed into the wall above her head.

Leilani rolled to the right, scattering herbs and cringing as the vial broke. A brass arm reached over the nearest crate. Gears clicked as a mechanical guard's face appeared above the boxes. Spinning eyes caught and recorded her crime. Another bolt whizzed past and she pressed against the wall to avoid being skewered.

A second automaton stood in the alley's mouth. This one's arm pointed in her direction. The hand hung from its hinge revealing a barrel that contained more wicked darts.

"Halt!" A mechanical order barked from the thing's belly. Xiang didn't bother fitting his hounds with proper mouths.

She counted her options. If Xiang was in a good mood, she'd only lose her hand. The roofline hung over enough to grab, but she didn't fancy taking a dart mid-leap. She stood. The first guard scrambled onto the top crate and jumped, landing on the cobbles in a clatter of brass widgets. Now he blocked the other's weapon, but Leilani still stood within his reach.

"Halt! Surrender!"

She shuffled backward. The automaton mirrored her movements, its joints squeaking. When she reached the end of the alley her options disappeared. If Xiang was in a foul mood … Leilani sprang straight up. Her hands snagged the lip of the overhang. Heaving and kicking, she pulled her chest up onto the tiles. Her legs still dangled over, however, and cool fingers tightened around her ankle.

She pulled, but the metal fingers clenched and pain lanced up into her calf. She heard a bang below. A hiss rose up from the alley and she felt the heat of steam against her legs. The grip released. She flung her legs up and rolled onto the rooftop.

"Halt! Surrender!"

Another crash followed and then a clatter of metal. Leilani paused. She should take her good fortune and run. She would find enough trouble waiting at home.

"Hahtttttttttttt trenderrrrg."

She scooted back to the edge and peeked over. A dart whizzed below but she couldn't see its target. She *could* see the remains of one attacker. Its torso sprawled, wrenched open, spilling springs and gears across the cobbles. It still had one leg attached that kicked pitifully.

A whirl of fabric flipped into view. Another thunk answered along with a series of echoing, metallic blows. Leilani lay down and poked her head over the rim.

The second guard still stood on its feet but it wobbled and leaked steam at the joints. One of its arms hung from a single spring while its good arm waved violently. A strange man twirled in a swath of oversized garments and leapt half-way up the alley wall. He stepped effortlessly against the planks, flew toward the guard, and tore off its head with one kick.

Leilani dropped into the alley. Now that the stranger had stopped spinning, she could see enough to know he hadn't come from the island — not anywhere near the islands. He looked old country.

The garments he wore wrapped his body like a shroud, tucked into bindings at the wrists and ankles. His skin and eyes told her even more than his clothing — he'd come from overseas. He looked like Xiang had when he'd first stepped off the boat, before he'd grown fat on poi and the islanders' taxes.

She reached for the automaton's head and watched the stranger's eyes widen. "Their memories." She stabbed a shaking finger at the head. "There's a cylinder in the back." When he didn't respond, she moved again, tensed to spring away should he attack. She rolled the head over and probed the base of the skull with her fingers. The memory tube rested under the plates which she pried apart enough to pop the thing out. She laid it on the ground and stood. The stranger might have been a statue.

Leilani crushed the cylinder with her heel and eyed the second guard's remains. She looked at the head, already partly cracked open, then at the stranger beside it, then back to the head. If she could crush both cylinders, she might avoid a beating.

She sidled toward the wreckage, keeping her eyes on the man. His head tilted. Leilani squatted, tore out the memory tube, and ground it into the cobblestones. Only one witness and she had a feeling he wouldn't run to tell Xiang.

"Why do you steal?"

Leilani stood taller and stuck out her chin. "I only take a pinch each time."

"A pinch of dishonesty can start a landslide of sorrow."

"Right. Well, thanks for the warning and," she waved toward the metal bodies, "that, but I really should get back."

He moved fast. One minute he leaned against the wall and the next he stood right beside her. He brushed the hair off her face. Leilani turned away but not before he saw the bruises.

"He beats you."

"It could be worse."

His eyes narrowed. "A man who dishonors women is no man at all."

"Sure." Leilani backed out of his reach and then turned to face the alley mouth. One step and a rustle of silk and he landed in front of her.

"Yi!" She clutched at her chest and shook her head. "How do you move like that?"

"I'm looking for someone." This time the twitch turned into a sly smile. "A man named Xiang."

She looked over his shoulder, beyond the alley entrance to Kamehameha Bay sparkling under the Hawaiian sun. Three ships moored there and she guessed he'd come on the newest. Leilani didn't know what might make a man cross an ocean to find Xiang but she knew enough about Xiang to guess it wasn't pleasant.

"Just go up the hill." She turned to the rise above the town and pointed toward the apex. "The highest spot. You can't miss it."

He dipped into a bow so crisp that she flinched.

"Well, thanks again, and good luck with, whatever."

"Vengeance."

"Nice."

Leilani left the alley at a trot. She scuttled across the street and down along the curving shoreline. If her eyes darted to the ship a time or two, who could blame her? The new arrival had multiple square sails and a hull like dragon's scale. Curved beams poked out like spines along its bow, and the crew all wore the manner and the garments of the old country.

Not her country. Leilani's coloring and hair gave her away as a native though she wore the short pants and shirt of any shop study. Her thick, black hair and skin brown like a coconut shell marked her.

Mene's apothecary operated from the cheaper side of the street, without beach access. Leilani crossed the street where black lava stretched out into the sea. She hurried up the path between rickety buildings as the air fogged with the steam venting around laundry windows. She ducked the plumeria bushes and scurried to Master's front door.

The knob triggered a lever that sent a whistle screeching through the dark shop. She cringed when it howled but pressed on. The rafters hung with bundles of herbs and animal parts. The shelves along each wall overflowed with pouches, glass vials, boxes and leather bags, and the whole shop smelled of armpit.

"Late!" Mene bellowed from the papasan behind the low counter. The wicker creaked as he shifted his bulk around to fix her with a furious glare. "Always late from the market." His fat arm flicked in her direction and she ducked on reflex. The dowel clattered against the door behind her. "Bring that back."

She snatched up the wooden dowel and carried it to the counter, setting it on the glass top without stepping into range of his fists. Even so, she moved back a pace before retrieving the packets from her pockets. She laid them in a line, one at a time, while he read the labels. His lips flapped as he mumbled the powders' names. She held her breath when he stopped and tensed for the blow.

"Dragon's blood?"

"I — I dropped it, Master."

His lips twisted, but his eyes dropped to the shelves below the counter. "Xiang is holding a luau." He leaned forward and reached into the case. "He's ordered fresh amulets. One of each."

She exhaled and nodded. Her shoulders settled and she leaned one elbow on the countertop. Mene pulled out a parcel. He placed it on the counter and untied the string.

"Protection from fire." He peeled away the paper and lifted the first pouch. "Protection from flood." He removed them one at a time, lifting the thongs from which the talismans would dangle around Xiang's neck. "Disease, Assassins, Impotence. Protection from demons and hostile magic."

Leilani leaned toward the scent of herbs and inhaled. She could make these pouches in her sleep but still, they fascinated her.

She shouldn't have relaxed, but Mene had known she would. She leaned a fraction closer and the back of his hand smacked her face hard enough that she stumbled away. Blood filled her mouth and she blinked against instant tears.

"Seven pouches," he continued as if nothing had happened. "You will take them to Xiang and you will not *drop* anything along the way." He sniffed and rewrapped the bundle. "Clean yourself up first. I won't have you showing up on the hill like that."

Leilani nodded. She pressed one hand against her mouth to stop the blood and looked out under a curtain of tears and long, black, islander hair. "Yes, Master."

Xiang's complex squatted at the top of the island's first rise. The volcano towered behind it, but the town, the wharf, all of his domain lay below, along the waterfront, where he could keep an elevated eye upon it.

Leilani stepped out of the rickshaw with the parcel hugged tight against her chest. The complex lawns teemed with islanders and Chinese alike. Brown men with twists of fabric around their bottoms slithered up palm trunks to fetch coconuts. Women in muumuus beat taro in the courtyard, their chatter filling the air as much as the banging of the roots. Leilani wandered amongst them, keeping her eyes on the pair of metal guards at either side of the carved wooden doors.

The outer buildings employed palm, tapa and wicker in traditional island fashion but the central fortress swooped with ceramic tiles and dragon-shaped finials. The automatons clicked and whirred as she passed but made no move to stop her.

A tiled hallway ringed Xiang's audience chamber and an advisor met her here, sneering behind a thin string of mustache.

"You are the apothecary woman?"

"Yes. I have Master Xiang's amulets."

"Wait here."

Leilani sat on a stone bench. Her lip throbbed and she licked it and closed her eyes. Her lacquer belt almost held enough herbs. She could start her own apothecary but it needed to be far away from Mene.

Something clattered against the tiles. She sat up straight and turned to the left. The empty corner stared back at her but she *had* heard something. Leilani stood and tiptoed down the hallway. She followed the inner wall and peeked around the corner.

An automaton lay in pieces a few feet from her. Farther down, she saw the outline of a second. Squinting, she focused on the shadows at the end of the hall. They moved, dark against dark, billowing like twisting silk. The word echoed in her memory, *vengeance*. Leilani stepped into view.

The shadow froze. His eyes widened in surprise.

"Does he deserve it?" Her breath slipped in and out, and her heart pattered.

"For my sister." His voice held steel.

Leilani nodded and watched him vanish. She couldn't risk any further delay. Her feet scampered back to the bench, and her mind chewed furiously on a plan of action.

"Flood and Fire?" Xiang poked at the pouches with his cane. "Did he get them all?"

"They all seem to be here." The advisor glowered at Leilani.

"Well, pass them over."

Xiang's throne sat on a raised step and his long cane tapped the pouches until the advisor scooped them up. Leilani knelt on the floor, head down. Her eyes drifted from the huge braziers that burned all around the throne to the corners where shadows danced.

Xiang looped the amulets around his neck. In the firelight, his tattoos undulated against leathery skin. His fingers curled and uncurled as the advisor passed over her Master's magic. Demons, hostile magic, seven amulets of protection.

"Better!" Xiang bellowed, patted the amulets, and waved an arm in her direction. "You may go."

She scuffled across the room and up two steps to the exit. She kept her eyes away from the one shadow that moved against the others. Four steps across the hallway and she slunk between the automatons. Two steps into the courtyard and she heard Xiang howl. Metal crashed in the distance and guards raced to the audience chamber.

Leilani hurried through the outer gates, veered right and scurried around the back. She hid behind a palm trunk by the rear wall of the fortress where, inside, Xiang battled his assassin with six amulets and one empty pouch around his neck.

A plume of smoke blossomed above the building. Screams floated from the courtyard. Leilani held her breath and witnessed the silk-swathed figure spring over the wall. He landed in a crouch and looked to either side, smiling when he saw her waiting. Her fingers tugged the amulet into view and he laughed.

"Would it have helped him?" She held her breath.

"A pinch of dishonesty..."

"A landslide of sorrow," she finished for him. He hadn't said whose sorrow.

"Your lip is bleeding." He frowned.

"You may have trouble getting back to your ship."

"Perhaps."

"There's a bigger port in Hilo." She pointed inland toward the road that wound to the far side of the island. Hilo was far enough from Mene but the journey would be too dangerous by herself.

"You would travel alone with a strange man?"

"A man who would dishonor a woman is no man at all."

She thought he'd argue. Instead, he nodded and bolted like a dart through the trees. He'd be hard to keep up with, her stranger.

She tucked the pouch back into her shirt — protection from assassins — and ran after him.

Frances Pauli was born and raised in Washington State. She grew up with a love of reading and storytelling, and was introduced to Science Fiction and Fantasy at an early age through the books kept and read by her father.

Seeds of the Lotus

Camille Alexa

I bow low as I can, brow brushing the same floor that kisses Madame One Ming's embroidered slippers where they dangle limply off the edge of Her mockwood dais. Thinking of this, I lift my forehead the width of a Martian sand-mite's tentacle off the floor, my cloned skin unworthy of touching the ground where She has walked.

The gong rings twice and Madame's housedroid announces my presence with its old-fashioned protocol, as it does every day: "Lotus Blossom Sixty-three."

Even by Martian standards the droid is an ancient model, boxy and dull, the heads of its square rivets worn nearly flat, the door to its furnace ill-fitting. Its copper vocalizers are far older than my vat-grown bones, its voice atonal and tinny as steam spurts involuntarily from its vents with the wheeze of tiny bellows. Not raising my head, I shuffle forward on my knees toward the polished mockwood dais until the embroidered toes of Madame One's slippers come into view. The shiver I always feel in Her presence zips along my spine, delicious tremors shaking the tips of my fingers, the ends of my looping braids.

"Rise, little lotus blossom," says Madame, beautiful hand extended for my kiss. Careful not to disturb the golden casings on the nails of Her third and fourth fingers, I kiss, then rise. Her face is porcelain-perfect, lines smoothed under thick white powder, lower lip scarlet with the rouge I make from the pulverized ores of our red planet.

She caresses my cheek with one long nail. Its golden point is sharp and lovely where it creases my skin. "My blossom," She says, "our minedroids report Jacob Tinker's wagon approaching from the east."

I step back in surprise. "Two days early! And he approaches from the west! Always from the west!" The rhythm of the old trader's circuit is as central to my understanding of time as is the sun setting each night on our curved dome and Madame One's cricket automaton chirping each morning in its terracotta pot. I mark my months by the trader's arrival and departure, all twelve arrivals and departures since the day after I opened my eyes to the world, fully formed from the vat, and Madame One Ming bestowed Her first glorious kiss onto my cheek.

Madame smiles at me, places a soothing hand on my head. "Well this time, little blossom, he approaches from the east, and today."

"Yes, Madame One Ming." I scrape low and back from the chamber.

Out in the rocky courtyard, halfway between Madame's pagoda and the airlock pavilion with its gaping dragon jaw gate, I pause to draw a deep breath of recycled air. Overhead the sky is glorious, shot with threads of deeper red against the familiar orange haze. Light filters through to glance off the curving glassy surface of our dome, the sun a ripe round fruit hanging heavy in the sky, as delicious as the tangerine the trader brought once, shipped all the way from Moon. I love that sun, love that sky, almost as much as I love Madame.

Dust is thick in the air today. The trader's wagon is practically at the dragon gate before I see it, even with my gene-modified sight. Our three cylindrical minedroids clunk clumsily in the wagon's wake, their long metal queues swinging stiffly behind them. Each carries its satchel of ammonium salts, the fuel which feeds their metal bellies and Dome II's sole trade good of any value.

The droids escort the wagon through the airlock, and the shimmery portable oxygen field around the conveyance pops like soap bubble from Madame's bath. I bow perfunctorily to the wagoner before rushing to fondle his clonemule's ears. The animal huffs gently into my palm, nuzzles my wrist hoping for a treat I do not have to give him.

"He likes you, Lotus," says the old man as he unhitches the beast. "I need to talk to the boss lady about a slight … complication. Is Nelumbo around?"

At Madame One's sacred name, I drop into an automatic kowtow. "She who Observes the Heavenly Rituals with a Solemn Fate, with Blessed Health, who Initiates Kindness with Extreme Talented Insights, Admires the Arts, with Great Virtue and with a Holy Appearance awaits you in Her pagoda, honored visitor."

The old wagoner puts his hand on my head, a gesture reminiscent of Hers. I sneak a peek at his face, see he's smiling at me. "All right, little Lotus," he says, speaking around the mockwood matchstick he carries clamped between his teeth. "All right."

From the rear of the wagon where the minedroids have begun unloading the foodstuffs Madame and I depend on, the glass tube replacements for our water still, the nourishment powders for our lichen crop, comes a roar: "Ding dong dang-it-all! Keep yer tincan hands to yer dang self! I ain't no sack of potaters!"

I go taut with surprise at the sound of another human voice and without conscious thought leap into Listening Crane stance. Genetic programming makes my muscles coil with Tiger strength. My hearing hones to painful acuity and my hands go rigid, a warrior's weapons, ready to kill with Thousand Deaths precision. The minedroids careen into confusion mode, their dented brass torsos clanking into each other as they stumble back, their pendulum queues of braided silver swinging from their hollow brainpans.

"Easy, Lotus," says the trader. "That's just my *complication*. Matty, come meet—" he pauses, squints at me, "—Lotus Blossom Sixty ... three." He sucks the matchstick in his mouth as a red-headed girl jumps from the wagon. She has only two braids, worn long rather than looped, each prickled with short blunt lengths of yellow straw. Her clothing is not the occidental bustles and lace petticoats from Madame's descriptions of Dome City ladies nor the regal embroidered gowns favored by Herself, but like a man's, loose and rough, with pointed stovepipe boots and pearly snaps for buttons. She's barely taller than I.

This is the fifth human I have seen in my year of life, and the only girl. Madame One is as far above me as the stars, and the old wagoner and other men who come from time to time to negotiate business with Her as unlike me as the minedroids or the wheezing housedroid. Only the clonemule has ever struck me as a creature similar to myself — the clonemule, and the dozen lotus seeds in the Walled Pavilion of Bright Symmetry, sleeping in their vats of copper and glass.

The girl claps straw from her hands and strides to me. When I do not alter my stance, she grabs one of my hard-angled hands from where it is poised for a Strike of the Snake, and pumps my stiff arm up and down, up and down. "Pleased to meet'cha," she says. Her smile is wide, her teeth many and white.

The trader nods. "You girls get acquainted while I go talk to the boss lady. Lotus, think your minedroids can show Echo here where to oil up? It's dusty out there."

He does not wait for an answer, but nods as though I've spoken and sets out across the courtyard toward Madame's pagoda. The girl drops my hand and, voice stabbing into my ears like a Hooked Claw of Persimmon Piercing, calls over her shoulder, "Come on, Echo! She ain't gonna bite you."

Distracted by the girl, I have failed to notice the mandroid. He approaches upright on his lower appendages, sleek and beautiful. He is the shiniest object I have ever seen, rounded and silver and perfect. His spherical gold eyes swivel to me.

"Lotus Sixty-three," says the girl, "this here's the Echo 3000 model my daddy done sent with me all the way from Luna Colony."

Never before have I been tempted to knock the floor for a droid, but something in the Echo's gaze pierces deep into my chest. He is a warrior, like me. I sense it.

I bow to him and he watches with orbs gold as the tips of Madame's nails. The girl grabs my hand again and swings me toward the main pagoda's tiled entryway. "Sure is pretty here in Dometown Eye-Eye," she says, face lit like rare-glimpsed dawn. "Way prettier than Dometown Icks. And don't even get me started about that nasty old Dometown Eye-Vee. If'n I never see that place again in my life it'll be too soon. Ain't that right, Echo?"

"Yes, Matty Johnson."

The Echo 3000's voice is smooth and modulated, nothing like Madame's housedroid with its flatulent wheezes and groans through vents predating the first human footfall on Mars. And of course the minedroids have no voice boxes at all, only coded dot-and-dash strikes against their torsos with their spade-like appendages best suited to shoveling ammonium salts into their belly furnaces. I glance over my shoulder as I'm dragged across the courtyard, watch the Echo 3000 stare after the girl who does not look back. The minedroids ring him like barrel-shaped satellites, small by comparison, their riveted appendages clumsy and indelicate as they tap their hammered brass torsos at him with tentative, respectful, mute inquisition.

The trader emerges from Madame One's pagoda as we mount the steps. I drop the boyish girl's hand and bow. "Thank you, honored visitor, for bringing Madame One Ming ground pearls and jade for Her longevity tea. Also, thank you for letting me pet your mule."

From beneath my lowered lashes I see kindness in his face, mingled with an elusive sadness. "You take care of yourself, Lotus," he tells me around the edges of his matchstick. To the girl he says, "Go easy on her, Matty."

I imagine her head popping under my foot with a Fluttering Heron attack, or her jaw rupturing as my fist hit home with a Closed Chrysanthemum blow. "No one need go easy on me, honored one," I say, watching the girl from the corner of my eye to see if she hears the steel in my voice.

He seems on the edge of more words, but only nods and pats my head before plodding to the airlock and his sweet little mule. The Matty girl runs after him, hugs him tightly before letting go. The Echo takes a step toward her but she waves him off with a laugh and an admonishment to "make new friends." She runs back to my side and he watches her with his gold spheres, watches her as she grasps me again and sweeps me into Madame's pagoda. Even after the hinged spirit wall slides into place behind us I feel him watching still, the flimsy synthetic material no match for the focus of his will.

The gong sounds and I kowtow to Madame One Ming. "Lotus Sixty-three," drones the housedroid, "and…." It sputters to a stop, its outmoded program struggling to assimilate new data. The Matty girl does not kowtow, but strides past me to Madame's dais, hand extended. Before she can touch Madame I launch into One Arrow Flying, tackle her from behind so we both sprawl to the polished tiles. She scrambles to her feet, assuming a fighting stance not recognizable to my genetic encoding, fists raised in clunky mimicry of Closed Chrysanthemum. I ease into Listening Crane pose, balancing on one foot, hands like deadly claws angled to the floor. I will tear this girl's eyes from her head with Imperial Plum Pluck. I will twist the dusty red braids out at their roots with a three-finger Radish Tug. If she tries to touch Madame again, I will—

"Enough!" At the displeasure in Her voice, I fall instantly to my knees and knock my head three times to the floor. "Lotus Sixty-three, this girl is our honored guest."

Madame never calls me by my number. Never. Tears sting my eyes, though the scrolls say my enhancements render this impossible.

Madame beckons with a long, gold-tipped nail. "Girl, come here."

With a glare at me, the girl tugs her shirtfront straight and mounts the mockwood dais. She stops short at the sight of Madame One Ming's talons and bows her head, not graceful at all. "Right pleased to meet you, ma'am," she says. "You sure got you a nice dome here, way nicer than Icks or Eye-Vee. Nicest place I ever seen, even back home at Luna Colony. Nicer even than Old Aunt Mazy the banker's wife's, and she gots her a real oak settle imported all the way from Earth, not even synthawood."

Madame smiles as though this inane chatter is not beneath Her notice. "Good fortune, prosperity, and longevity to you," She says, and turns to me. "Blossom, please fetch tea. Our visitor must be thirsty after her travels."

I knock the floor three times, perhaps too rapidly for proper humility, and hurry from the room. The girl is telling stories in her outlandish accent of Martian desert kraken, of kidnappings, of dancehall droids with immodest programming and garish petticoats — all tales of beyond Dome II, where I have spent my life and where Madame has spent much longer than that.

Banging cupboards in the Nine-Dragon kitchen pavilion, I try not to wonder how long the new girl will stay. At least a month and two days; that's how long before Jacob Tinker returns on his regular circuit. As water boils in its patterned iron kettle I duck into the alcove and light a precious incense stick, and entreat Madame's human ancestors to grant me strength not to kill our honored visitor before sunset.

Returning with the tray I find Madame laughing — *laughing!* — at some inanity about cloned cattle and their indelicate genetically modified undercarriages. Madame forgets even to smile at me when I kneel by Her slippers to watch Her whisk tea.

"...And so Echo and me, we hid in Granpappy Tinker's wagon under enough hay to feed Old Neddy the Goatman's entire herd back on Luna, and he took us a slight detour and brought us here. Said you was a real nice lady, used to be married to the richest man on Mars, who was supposed to be my kin, 'cause I was supposed to marry his youngest son's youngest, but that didn't work out so good…."

Thank Madame's human ancestors, the girl seems to have run out of air at last. She sits, legs crossed, one braid lifted to her mouth with the thoughtlessness of nervous habit. Madame scoops tea into a jade bowl. "I too came to Mars as a bride. A girl no older than you, no bigger than this little lotus blossom here." She turns Her gaze on me and my heart swells with radiance. "In my eyes, my future husband was not the richest man on Mars, but a young glassblower's apprentice from my childhood village."

The redheaded girl is still now, rapt and quiet. "You came from Earthside?"

Madame nods, picking up the ancient wooden whisk. "From farm country, like you. I'd only glimpsed Kun Li Cantrell as a little girl, by the well, scooping water into his experimental glass globes. Or at market, carrying his sealed spheres of water with bright goldfish inside, explaining to anyone and everyone how fish had to carry their atmosphere with them wherever they went, so they could breathe. But then he perfected his glassine compound, and the first domed city of Mars was born."

Madame has never told me so much of herself! So entranced am I, picturing Madame young and happy, momentarily I forget to loathe the redheaded girl. Without noticing, I have shifted my posture, and so has she. We kneel shoulder to shoulder before Madame like two students before our teacher.

"But then you came here, like? And married Mister Cantrell and had lots of babies?"

I should crush her in the Clamp of the Dragon for her disrespectful outburst, but Madame merely shakes Her head. *Whisk whisk*, goes the tea. *Whisk whisk*. "He had honored our little village in asking us to send him a bride. Few girls wanted to venture across an ocean of space just to marry a glassblower's apprentice. But I remembered the goldfish, and I remembered him juggling his glass spheres by the well." Madame One's eyes have gone soft, soft as when She drinks the special tea She never lets me even sip, or smokes that same tea in Her red clay pipe. "I'd completed my genetic reconditioning and training at the Steel Jade School, and thought my fight skills might be useful on a frontier planet. Even if they weren't useful, at least I was strong, and able to endure much physical hardship. And my skills were embedded in my genetic coding, to be passed to offspring. I felt ready for anything."

Unable to contain myself, I bow and kiss Her slippers three times in rapid secession. "Oh, Madame One! If only you still had the use of your poor legs, you could do anything still!"

Madame smiles. "Thank you, my lotus blossom. But there was a thing I could not do: I could not give my husband a son or daughter. It was what he wanted more than anything else in all the worlds, and the one thing the surgeons eventually told me I could never, never do. When we discovered this, I left Kun Li, brought my few androids — antiques by Earth standards even then — and my lotus seeds, and trekked across the red dunes of Mars to make a new home. I wanted him to be free, you see. Free to send for other women, who might provide what he desired more than everything in all the celestial heavens combined."

The Matty girl is counting on her fingers, murmuring numbers as she calculates. "But it's been..." she points to her fingers as though to an abacus showing a tally, "...that's nigh on ninety years since Mr. Cantrell settled here."

Madame sets aside Her bowl and whisk. Her cinnabar bracelets clack together as She reaches for the tiny porcelain cups. "And I've been here for eighty-two: the first twenty in Dometown Prime with my husband, and the last sixty-two without him. I did not even tell him when I fell ill shortly after leaving his city, and the desert wasting sickness left me without use of my legs."

You have me, Madame One! I want to cry. *You have me!* But knowing tonight is the anniversary of my birth keeps me silent. At least Madame has the lotus seeds. Enough lotus seeds for the last sixty-three years, and still a dozen more.

A sad and heavy silence settles in the room as Madame pours three cups of tea. The only sounds are of tea splashing, and the housedroid gently wheezing as he stokes his belly furnace with internal bellows growing thin and brittle, and behind it all a music so constant, it is the never-ending backdrop against which I experience the rest of the world — the patter of grit blowing against the surface of our glassy dome, red and relentless, the sands of Mars.

After tea the housedroid rings the gong four times, signaling the minedroids to bring the palanquin. In moments their clanging and bonging — they are not graceful beings — echoes across the courtyard. They enter, the Echo 3000 close behind. His golden orbs swivel to every corner of the room, observing all as a true warrior should. I wonder how I feel about him being present for the blossoming of a new seed. Wonder if I feel anything at all.

We are unaccustomed to outsiders, Madame and I. She nods with regal graciousness when the Echo 3000 steps to lift Her onto the palanquin. I might wish the Matty girl had not arrived on this exact day, but it's not as though I've lived this past year thinking anything in particular about the blossoming of a new lotus; I'm happy Madame has us to keep Her company, to keep Her safe. To love Her.

It's obvious the redheaded girl has more questions than there are pleats in a folded paper flower, but she keeps her silence as our procession wends across the courtyard. She cranes her neck, studying in open admiration the red clay tiles of the Nine-Dragon Pavilion, the peaks of Madame's pagoda, the rocks of the garden. Inside I feel an unfolding, a warmth and generosity toward her. Perhaps she can help the new lotus with the dry pebble creek I have been building for Madame, where She can see it from Her divan out Her window with the sunrise.

The Walled Pavilion of Bright Symmetry is not our grandest structure, but it is our largest. Long and low, it does not boast the decorative tiered roofs of the other buildings, nor the color-ful reds and oranges and pinks I mix from ores the minedroids collect at my instruction along with their ammonium salt fuel. Inside walls a meter thick, it is dark and cool, kept so for the sake of the seeds. I draw air into my lungs, hold it, and for a few beats of my modified heart let the peacefulness of the sinking sun wash through me. The horizon past our dome is perfect, the wind having ceased its howling and its blowing for once. The sky is that perfect tangerine color, a color which soaks into your skin and fills you from the inside, ripe and good.

Madame One Ming's android bearers shuffle the palanquin to the nearest lit tank. Darkened empty vats stand in rows behind like terracotta soldiers in an ancient Earthside tomb. Numbers stamped deep into the copper are readable even in the gloom: *63 ... 62 ... 61 ... 60 ... 59 ... 58....*

A startled gasp escapes our honored visitor. She goes to the nearest upright tank of soft gleaming copper. I have polished that copper every day this past year, have kept its rivets free of corrosion, have gently dabbed condensation from the glass window she reaches now to carelessly wipe with her dusty sleeve.

All my generous feelings of a moment ago are gone in an eyeblink. "No!" I shout, and fling myself at her with Drunken Monkey Off the Vine. Quick as a blink, a metal cable lashes out. *Whip whip whip* — that smooth segmented cable wraps my torso three times, plucking me from the air and preventing my two-pronged attack of One Fist Flying and Unlucky Bending Eel. The Echo 3000 retracts his telescoping arms slowly, drawing me to his side with unexpected gentleness. His beautiful gold orbs study my face and limbs, scanning for visible damage to my soft tissues.

"It's all right, blossom," says Madame, "she meant no disrespect. Matty, might your mandroid help Lotus Sixty-three up onto my palanquin? Her legs will be feeling weak."

Of course that's why my attack was so easily foiled; it has begun, slid upon me without my even noticing.

The Echo carries me to Her side to deposit me on the embroidered synthetic silks of the piled blankets and shawls. Lotuses. The pattern of Madame's embroidery is always of the lotus, which I have seen a thousand times and never thought upon too deeply.

"But there's tons of girls here!" says Matty. "I been wandering around, wondering where to find other girls like me, and here's one, two, three … at least ten of 'em sleeping right here."

"Twelve left," says Madame. "Twelve beautiful lotus seeds, one blossom maturing each year to replace that from the year before."

My arms have suddenly gone numb, but I barely notice in my rapture at Madame arranging Her silks around my face, propping my shoulders with Her own pillow so I might watch the tank with the number after mine, where Lotus Seed Sixty-four, pre-programmed consciousness now ripe and ready to blossom, slumbers in her luminescent amber fluid. Small bubbles rise from tubes snaking past the seed's naked shoulders, through the floating tendrils of her coal-dark hair, between her tight-closed lips.

Matty staggers back from the vat, swallowing hard, looking as if she might be sick on the smooth clay floor of the Walled Pavilion of Bright Symmetry. "That's so … so *horrible*."

She studies Madame with a disrespectful look I do not care for. Me, she does not look at, nor the Lotus in the vat. With a last glance at me and a motion of his telescoping upper appendage suspiciously like a caress to my cheek, the Echo 3000 moves to her side, supports her as he had me when my legs began to go.

"Are you comfortable, my blossom?" Madame asks. At my drowsy nod, She says to the girl, "It is not horrible. It is life. The gnat, the cricket, the woman, the sacred golden carp in the pool of a goddess: an hour, a season, a century, a millennium. My blossoms have all the life the surgeons could give them at the time of their creation; one year is all any of the old clones had, once they emerged from the vat. But a year is an eternity to the butterfly. Would you have these seeds destroyed, never to see the light of Martian day? That would be far more horrible, I think. Too horrible for me, though my husband urged it. This was my effort to give him the many children he so desired. But he said it would be like watching me die, every year for the rest of his life."

She gazes into my face with what I now see is Her love. Her love burns as bright for me as mine has always burned for Her. No; brighter.

Receiving Her look of love, almost worship, I wonder: *Is this how it feels to be Madame?* I've never put myself in Her delicious embroidered slippers before, never thought myself worthy. Now, swaddled in Her silks as the sun dips at last below the horizon and the room grows even dimmer, Madame's bone-thin arms around me, I feel closer to Her than I ever have, feel at last that connection the scrolls say exists in the very genetic coding of a clone's bones, along with her preprogrammed martial talents and the color of her eyes.

"I'm from you, Madame," I say, feeling the wonder of it. "I'm made of bits of you, as though I were real."

She smoothes my hair from my cheek. "You are real," She says. "My beautiful darling blossom. My lovely little lotus."

Matty slumps against the Echo 3000, hides her face against his silvery torso as he wraps his upper appendages around her shoulders. The minedroids have withdrawn to stand with the housedroid in a formation of respect I have read about in scrolls, but never seen. Something stirs in the vat. "Oh, look, Madame!" I say. "The seed, she blossoms! Her eyes are opening."

But Madame doesn't look away from my face. A warm drop soaks the silk near my ear, a rivulet in Her white powder where tears wend a path across Her cheek. "Yes, my dear, my beautiful darling child. My child, my baby. Her eyes are opening."

Camille Alexa lives in the Pacific Northwest down the street from a volcano. Her stories appear in *Fantasy Magazine, Alfred Hitchcock's Mystery Magazine,* and *Imaginarium 2012: The Best Canadian Speculative Writing.* Her book *PUSH OF THE SKY* earned a starred review in *Publishers Weekly* and was an Endeavour Award finalist.

The Ability of Lightness

Tim Reynolds

"Watch me 'painting a rainbow', Quon!" Twelve-year-old Yu raised his arms up in curves, his hands above his shoulders, then brought his right hand over his head, turned his head to the left and brought his left arm down and out to the side, palm up. Looming above him, its neck stretched nearly up to the roof of the massive cavern, the giant brass and steel, clockwork Feilong steam-dragon watched without judgement. The mechanical flying beast's boiler was silent and its marvellous wings folded in and back, but it still dominated the cavern beneath the Galden Namgey Lahtse Monastery, waiting impassively, ready to fly at the hands of the Cloud Monks in defence of the People against the tyrants of the world.

Yu's younger brother, Quon, didn't even look up from the long wooden workbench he stood at. "Yah, yah, Yu. You're painting a fat little rainbow while I'm being a genius. Your stupid t'ai ji might make Master Wei nod and smile but when he inspects the graduates today and sees me and my steam-driven dragon-steppers display perfect Qinggong, light-stepping across the monastery rooftops, he'll accept me as his personal student and take me away to Lhasa to be the greatest Warrior Cloud Monk ever. I hope. If this thing works." He tightened the final brass nut and tugged on the thin copper pipe to test the strength of the new bracket.

"Of course it will, Quon. In only three weeks, you took all those spare dragon parts and made that machine. I just wish I was smart like you." Yu was a year older than Quon, a Rabbit to Quon's Dragon, but he was perfectly happy to follow his younger brother's lead. "You should try t'ai ji quan, Quon. Come here and follow me. It's really relaxing and you *really* need to relax."

"I don't have time for that silliness. Master Wei only visits once every ten years and he won't be back in Tawang Town until 1899, the Year of the Pig. By then, it will be too late. It has to be today or never."

Yu leaned and pushed, moved and pivoted, 'scooping the sea'. "You haven't even tested that thing, Quon. Maybe you should." He finished by 'looking at the horizon' and stepped over to make a closer inspection of Quon's invention. "Will it really make you dragon-step? How does it work? I see an old pair of boots, some really big springs and stuff, and that looks like a tiny boiler, like the one on the horseless wood-wagon or even the dragon." He reached out to touch a polished brass strut but Quon slapped his hand away.

"No! You just break things. Go 'separate the river' or something, while I finish up. The Graduation Call-to-Arms should sound any minute."

"I thought we were going to have breakfast first. I'm starved." In spite of his hunger, though, Yu started his movement by 'raising his arms', and then followed the sequence their Cloud Monk brother, Jung, had taught him. He moved gracefully in and around the giant Feilong dragon, smiling as the flickering lamplight reflected off thousands of hand-hammered scales. As he finished up by 'balancing the qi to a close', a large-bossed gong sounded. "Perfect timing! I feel balanced and calm and even a little lighter on my feet."

"Good for you, Round Ass. You need to lose weight. Now hold the cart so I can load up my dragon-steppers. Please." Quon scrambled to shift his pair of contraptions into a hand-cart. "Just think, Yu, by the end of today, you will be known all across the Tawang-chu Valley as the brother of Master Wei's newest student. That should at least get you a small discount in the marketplace."

"A discount would be good, especially when I take over the farm from father." Yu kept a firm grip on the cart's handles while Quon finished loading and then draped a bright red blanket over everything.

Quon tucked in the corners of the blanket and stepped back to inspect the load. "Perfect." He led the way out and Yu followed along, faithfully using his brawn to see his brother's dream come true. "We have ten minutes to get to the kakaling entrance gate, Yu. The ceremony will be in the courtyard so I'll dragon-step from the kakaling to the library and make one magnificent leap across to the Dukhang, the assembly hall. It will be a great moment in Cloud Monk history and I want you to be there in the courtyard to make sure they all know who the steam-monk is. I'll make one final, huge, Qinggong jump down into the court to accept my place at Master Wei's side." He sighed to himself. "With luck."

Yu ignored Quon's last comment, certain his brother could do anything he set his mind to. Just before he closed the door behind him he heard Jung and the other Cloud Monks entering the cavern from the other side to prepare the steam-dragon for their daily sky patrol. He pushed the door shut as softly as he could and hurried after Quon.

The brothers arrived at the stone entrance gate just as the final gathering gong sounded. Quon gave Yu a light shove. "Go! Get to the courtyard! I can do this myself!"

"Are you sure you don't need my—"

"No! I need you in the courtyard! As soon as you get there start whispering my name. That way, when I leap over their heads, they will already be talking about me. Go! Go! Go!" Quon ripped the blanket off the cart and got to work assembling his device. Yu took off at a run just as a huge shadow passed over them. A quick glance up showed the Feilong dragon slowly gaining altitude above the monastery with Jung in the saddle.

Yu wound his way through the dozens of buildings until he reached the courtyard. There had to be at least a thousand people there, all dressed in their finest robes to honour both the newest Cloud Monks and Master Wei, brother of their very own Abbott, Master Keung. Yu jockeyed for a good view, working his way through the crowd, along the outside of the courtyard. He spied a nearly empty staircase and aimed for that vantage point, trying not to step on toes or knock over wobbly old-timers.

"Excuse me, pardon me, sorry." Halfway to the staircase he remembered Quon's instructions. "Where's Quon? Have you seen Quon?" he whispered loudly as he squirmed his way through the packed crowd. "I'm looking for Quon, have you seen my brother, Quon?"

An old woman jabbed an elbow in his ribs on his way past. "Shut up, boy! Master Wei is about to speak!"

"Sorry." He moved on as quickly as he could. By the time he reached the staircase and ran to the landing at the top, he was seriously short of breath. The day was hot, the crowd was massive, and the excitement was overwhelming. Yu took a deep breath to calm himself. He 'separated the clouds' and 'pushed the waves', focusing on his qi and not the buzzing crowd or the baking sun. He closed his eyes and tried to concentrate on Master Wei's voice like an island in the storm of bodies. He breathed in, and breathed out, and listened.

"Brothers and Sisters, thank you so much for your kind and generous welcome. It saddens me that my duties to the order keep me away and I can only find my way home every ten years. Much is changing in the world beyond our mountains, beyond blessed Tibet and India, so this place, this locus of peace, warms my heart greatly. Today is a very special day because it is the day we welcome new Cloud Monks to the order. My dear brother, Keung, has asked me to do the honour of introducing you to the newest warriors in the battle against oppression and slavery. But first, a prayer. O Amida, Oneness of Life and Light—"

A tremendous steam whistle, followed by a high-pitched, blood-curdling scream, interrupted the prayer. Yu opened his eyes just in time to see Quon bound, out of control, from the eastern rooftop to the western one. Quon appeared to have legs at least two feet longer than normal and when he landed on the far roof, his legs compressed and the still-building pressure shot him back up into the sky again.

Masters Wei and Keung both vaulted lightly up onto the steeply sloped tile roof of the Dukhang, running madly after the rocket boy. Without a second thought, Yu launched himself ten feet up onto the library roof, thinking only of his cousin's safety. He ran straight up to the peak, taking giant steps and doing his best not to slip. He watched as Quon blew past Master Keung and, although the Abbott leaped high, he was too late to reach him.

The dragon-steppers shot Quon straight down into the courtyard, forcing the crowd to run for the exits. Yu was sure that his little brother was going to hit the stones headfirst and be killed by his own invention, but at the very last moment Quon got his feet under him and the impact was absorbed. Master Wei changed directions suddenly and sprang down to the courtyard, but while the master was inbound, Quon's dragon-steppers released their pressure and blasted him sky-high like a New Year's rocket.

Yu shut down his fear, closed his mind to everything else, took a deep breath and flew straight up off the roof and into Quon's path. The young brothers crashed together and Quon's skinny little elbow slammed hard into Yu's head, but Yu held on tight. The dragon-steppers sputtered, and then ran out of steam. Yu smiled. It was over. Quon was safe. And then he looked down and saw they were nearly a hundred feet above the courtyard.

He was puzzled for a moment, having no idea how on earth they got so high, but his confusion was quickly forgotten when gravity started to drag them back down. He took a deep breath, focused his qi, and tried to remember everything he was taught. Then he heard the hiss of a massive steam engine below him and saw a glint of sunlight on brass and gold wings. "Jung!" Yu shouted, and he saw Master Wei leap from roof crest to dragon wing to arrow straight toward them. "You've saved us, Master! Quon! We're saved!"

No answer. Yu felt Master Wei's arms close around them. "Quon…?"

Yu looked back over his shoulder at the Tawang-chu Valley and straightened his pack.

"You are homesick already, young Yu?"

"No, Master Wei, just wondering how Quon will take to farming."

"It is only until he learns some discipline and his legs are healed. If he applies himself, he should be able to apply for the academy in two years' time."

"Will his legs ever heal completely? They're really smashed up."

"Not completely. I don't think he will ever master the ability of lightness in Qinggong, but after the three of us were swept out of the sky by Jung on the Feilong dragon, I think Quon has set his sights on flying. Only time will tell, though." He took a sip from his water skin. "Now, shall we make our way to Lhasa?"

"Of course, Master. Can I ask one question, though?"

"You may ask as many questions as you wish, Yu. You are with me to learn."

"Thank you, Master. So, when do we stop for lunch?"

Tim Reynolds is a Calgary, Alberta writer/photographer. In the past year he has had steampunk, fantasy, horror, romance, science fiction, and historical stories published. He received an Honourable Mention in the Writers of the Future Contest and is a proud member of the Imaginative Fiction Writers Association and SF Canada.

Fire in the Sky

Ray Dean

The rooster's call shook Wong Feng awake. After a quick stretch to loosen the stiffness in his back, he walked to town. There was much to do. And only a few short hours of daylight.

Here, the morning sun was bright but within the port town there was only the heavy grey light cast by the shifting shadows of airships floating just above the rooftops. If he had a choice he would never set foot in town again, but there was something he must see through. Feng stopped under a tree at the end of a street and looked up into its branches. He narrowed his gaze at the shadows above his head. There was no movement yet. A simple bang on the trunk shook leaves and startled a cry. A child of ten landed at his feet, eyes half-closed with sleep.

"Good morning, Little Xing."

Rubbing at his eyes, the boy looked at Feng with a rather indignant gaze. "You wouldn't say that if you'd slept in a tree for more than a week."

Feng ruffled the boy's hair. "Tell me what you've seen."

Little Xing crossed his arms over his chest. "I watch the airships and it's always the same. Come night the windows go empty except for the men on guard and most of them fall asleep once they're alone."

The news was good and it showed on Feng's face. He gave the boy a hearty tap on his back, sending him on his way.

When Feng reached Po's Paper Factory he was reminded of the terrible imposition that the British and their shipments had put upon the people of his town. A business that had once been housed in a neat two room building was now conducted beneath awnings of oil-cloth lashed to tree trunks. Milling crowds made it difficult to catch Po's eye. The older man finally found him at the edge of the crowd. "State your business, but don't waste my time, Feng. We have orders to fill and you," Po waggled a finger at him, "are little more than a distraction on a good day."

Feng brushed past Po, squeezed between the tables that crowded the floor and stopped where Su Yin assembled paper lanterns. "Tonight?" he whispered.

Su Yin kept her eyes on the paper lantern, fingers avoiding the sharp wires that created its shape. As she reached for another length of wire she rewarded Feng with the slightest hint of a smile.

The other girls giggled and Po's expression soured like old milk. "You girls go back to work!" He waved his hand, bringing Feng to his side just as a British soldier walked by, his buttons winking in the remnants of sunlight.

"We filled a number of orders yesterday." Po's forceful baritone, even softened to a whisper, drew Feng's attention. "This will be quite the surprise."

Feng's schooled his reaction to a simple nod. "It will. Are my deliveries ready?"

"Now that's the spirit. Get to work like the rest of us." Po's expression darkened as his eyes followed the soldier disappearing into the crowd. "Would you have thought this up if you still worked at the harbor?"

Feng tensed. He didn't like to talk about the past, how the airships had come and shut him out of work. "Something has to be done."

"If only the magistrate would do his job and enforce the laws," Po sighed, "we'd be rid of their cargo."

"The English found their way around them," Feng explained, the words scratching his throat, "the law says they can't bring opium into the harbor." The shifting light that slipped across the table tops drew his attention to the sky. Another airship marked with an English coat of arms was descending at the edge of town. "Because the airships can dock anywhere, they don't need to bring cargo into the harbor. I have no ships to offload."

Po leaned closer, his breath wheezing on Feng's cheek. "If they had left us our weapons, we'd face them man to man."

"Spears and swords?" Feng countered with a smile and a friendly hand on Po's shoulder. "We'd be dead in the street with bullets in our bodies and they'd just bring in their own customers for the pipe."

Su Yin wrapped bundles of folded lanterns in plain brown paper and tied them with string. Feng tucked the packages under his arm and left.

The second of his deliveries found him.

"Feng!" The laughing sound of his name came from Wu Shen. Appearing at his elbow like a ghost from the grey fog of bodies, Wu's bright smile was a welcome sight.

Feng sorted through his remaining packages.

"Later, later," Wu waved him off. "Come." Wu took his arm and led him into the crowd.

Feng murmured apologies to the men he jostled, bowing slightly again and again as they moved to the side of the street. "You fixed your rickshaw?"

"Fix? Why bother?" Wu waved as if he could send the very thought away like smoke. "Here," Wu swept out his hand in a grand gesture at his rickshaw. "Look!"

Feng looked under the rickshaw. The wheels were still broken and firmly stuck.

Wu had built an engine for his rickshaw to carry men and opium from the British airships to the dens. The innovation, its boiler and crank too heavy for his humble conveyance, buckled the rickshaw's wheels.

Now, the same engine that had earned irate words from his wife was hard at work. Sitting atop the boiler was a multi-layered steamer. At each joint, a steady curtain of steam escaped into the air and the smells that caused Feng's stomach to rumble promised that delicious bao was cooking inside.

"Ah!" Feng nodded. "Ingenious!"

Wu's wife slapped her husband's hand away from the cover. "We have paying customers!"

"I'm making deliveries." Feng reached into his pocket for some money. "I can pay for a bun." A moment later, he looked up sheepishly for his fingers found nothing but a few strings and a piece of lint.

"Come back when you can pay." Wu's wife turned on her husband, menacing him with bamboo tongs.

Feng handed a package to Wu and bowing to the wife, he backed into the crowd.

Behind his wife's back, Wu lifted the cover off the steamer. He drew out a bun, tossing it high over the crowd into Feng's outstretched hand.

If there was a slight shake to his hands Feng believed it could be forgiven. In the last few months he had eaten little and slept even less. He'd lost his job to the men who brought opium into China and he'd be damned before he succumbed to it himself. Deliveries done, he strolled to the Opera House. Soon, he would meet Su Yin.

The door was unlocked and he expected the Opera House to be empty giving him a quick access to the courtyard. It was just his luck that the British soldiers were having a party inside.

Rice wine bottles littered the table amongst playing cards and coins. The biggest man was the one with the most ribbons decorating his uniform. He pointed a heavy finger at Feng and said something that vaguely reminded Feng of a question.

When Feng only smiled, the man stood, nearly tipping the table and spilling coins to the floor. More words, and again, Feng smiled and nodded.

He felt many eyes on him and growing frustration. They had weapons and he — he had only his two hands and his wits, but he knew a thing or two about music.

The men watched him with caution as he removed a dusty tambur from the wall.

"It's quite simple," he spoke even though they didn't understand. "I'm here to cause trouble and I'm hoping you'll try to stop me."

Feng crossed to the door at the back of the room, his fingers drawing out a plaintive tune from the tambur.

Turning about, Feng knocked a soldier to the floor. The young man sputtered with outrage and looked about for help. Another soldier lunged and stopped for the end of the tambur was now tucked neatly under his chin. A sharp thrust and he was on the floor gasping for air.

One soldier staggered forward and managed to land a punch. Momentum more than skill lead to the lucky strike but Feng's foot tripped up the soldier, sending him sprawling into a stand of yunluo gongs. The reverberating crash disguised the advance of another man. Feng broke the tambur with a vicious snap and wrapped the strings around the man's neck, cutting off his breath. Another pushed Feng against the wall, his angry fists cutting through the air with crisp blows that snatched the air from Feng's lungs.

Feng's fingers found the solid wooden bow of a Jinghu fiddle and used it to play an entirely new instrument, eliciting shouts of pain from the soldier before tumbling him back onto the floor. The only sound from the soldier then was the hollow knock of his head.

The bow in Feng's hand looked as thin as a chopstick compared to the imposing figure of the last man. The soldier reached for Feng's wrist and missed, opening his body for another kind of attack. Feng jabbed the pressure points on the man's torso calling them out as he went. "Stomach, liver, kidney," the man turned green and Feng gave him a triumphant smile, "and bladder." The soldier crumpled to the floor.

Feng grinned. "I told you I came to cause trouble." He tapped on another fallen man's head with the bow and said, "Be good and stay here for a bit while I finish what I came to do."

In the cover of darkness Feng sneaked into the Opera House's courtyard. There had only been four ropes to untie and he finished in moments. That done, Feng scrambled up onto the roof of the Opera House.

Su Yin crouched on the tiles, her clothes dark like the night sitting heavily around them both. Feng knelt and touched her arm.

She started and covered his hand with her own. "The ropes?"

Feng nodded. "It only took a moment to untie them. The ship is moving. Look." He pointed to the airship before them in the ink-dark night. As they watched, the bulging hulk of canvas rose and drifted away from the town.

Su Yin produced a small flute and bringing it to her lips she mimicked the song of a nightingale. Across the rooftops others echoed her call. She dropped the flute back into her pocket with a smile. "The other lines have been untied."

Somewhere below, the noisome boiler of Liu's noodle factory blew its customary evening whistle and Feng turned to Su Yin.

"Light the candle."

Her touch disappeared into the darkness and a moment later a candle flickered, half hidden behind the gentle curve of her hand.

Holding the paper lantern's frame with one hand, Feng used the other to lift its delicate walls away from the wick. Su Yin lit the wick with the candle. They both sighed with relief when the flame caught and grew in size. The flame licked the air and slowly the lantern inflated, glowing with a warm cheery light.

Feng looked across the tiled and slanted rooftops, beyond the silver gilt of the moonlight, and saw scores of lanterns glowing in a field just beyond the town's edge. He knew once he let this lantern go there was no turning back. He waited, timing the position of the airships as they drifted toward the harbor.

When the last airship passed them by, a light appeared on its bridge. A face pressed against the window, eyes half-closed with sleep. Feng released the lantern and it floated up into the night, illuminating the face pressed against the airship's window; the man followed its path with a curious look. When the lantern passed safely by the skin of the airship he smiled, relieved that any danger had passed.

The lantern that rose from their rooftop had only been a signal. Now, the field stretching down to the harbor blossomed with light as hundreds of lanterns lifted into the air and swarmed about the loosed airships.

Fire licked holes in canvas skins and guards raised the alarm as burning ships drifted away from the town and over the harbor.

"What happens now?" Su Yin's eyes were wide as she watched airships flare like fireworks in the night sky. Her fingers tightened against his.

Feng knew her question was an honest one. There might be more ships. More soldiers. He took her hands in his, drawing her close.

"I don't know what they'll do, but they know that we'll find a way to fight."

Ray Dean was born and raised in Hawaii where she spent many a quiet hour reading and writing stories. Performing in theater and working backstage lead her into the delights of Living History. The genre of Steampunk allows her to play in a history created from her own imagination.

The Legend of Wong Heng Li

Frank Larnerd

Lying on his back with his straw hat pulled low, Wong Heng Li let the spring sun warm his bones. He was dreaming of home, of Zhu Yan, the bandit girl, and the baby she cradled in her arms.

In the dream, the baby reached for Wong, wrapping her tiny fingers around his thumb.

"Wake up," said a voice, cutting through the vision.

Frowning, Wong lifted the brim of his hat. "You called for lunch. I still have twenty minutes."

Boss Tanner put his hands on his hips. "You'll get your break. Now come on. There's a man I want you to meet."

Wong followed the rail boss past the tents to the front of the line. A colorfully painted wagon drawn by four dapple horses stood by the tracks. Next to the wagon was a spectacled man with an enormous curled mustache.

Tanner said, "Wong, say hello to Mr. Coppersmith."

"What about my break?" Wong asked.

"Listen," Boss Tanner said, taking Wong aside. "This fellow says he'll pay a hundred dollars if I got a man that can beat his machine. He's trying to impress the Central Pacific with my testimonial."

"Not interested."

Tanner grabbed his shoulder. "Come on, I'll split it with you. Seventy-thirty."

Wong brushed past him.

"I told you those coolies are too small to be efficient," Coppersmith said.

Wong wheeled around, his braid whipping about. "Chinese people might be small, Mr. Coppersmith, but remember, we made one giant wall." He turned to his boss. "Fifty-fifty."

Tanner licked his lips. "Sixty-forty?"

"Who helped you when the wolves came?"

"You did."

"And the Indians?"

"You did, Wong."

"And the Mormons?"

"Dammit, Wong." Tanner rolled his eyes. "Alright, fifty-fifty."

A half hour later, the entire camp gathered near the track they had prepared for the contest. Protruding from the timbers were rows of steel spikes, tapped in just enough to hold them upright. The railmen whispered to one another as Wong stretched beside the rails.

"Gentlemen," Mr. Coppersmith called out. "Today, you will witness the future of locomotive ingenuity. My latest design will usher in a new age, an age where machines not only replicate, but improve on man's labor. No longer will we be burdened with foreign hordes and their corrupting influences."

Wong spat in the dust.

"No. No, my good sirs," Coppersmith continued. "Let every soul here make note and spread the message of this demonstration far and wide. Tell your friends of the fateful day that you beheld the industrial ingenuity of Coppersmith Steam and Automation Designs as it drove the first blow in its destiny to hammer out the defects of mankind's pursuit of physical endeavors!"

Coppersmith yanked a lever attached to the wagon. "I give you Astondo! The metal man!"

Machinery clicked and groaned the sides of the carriage folded away.

Wong wrapped his braid around his neck as a giant shining statue climbed down from the wagon. It was ten feet tall and made of bronze metal plates. Broad at the shoulders, the machine had giant arms, one ending in a massive mallet, the other a three-fingered claw. Its face had simple stern features, and on its head was a spiked Prussian helmet.

Astondo lumbered toward the group, causing the rail workers to fall back before it.

Coppersmith smiled. "Astondo, are you ready to show these gentlemen what you're made of?"

Steam hissed from the machine's mouth as it twirled its mallet in the air.

Wong stood beside the bronze machine. Its head swiveled toward him and let out a menacing hiss.

Boss Tanner called to the competitors. "Before you is a hundred yards of track. Each of you will take a side, driving in every spike until you hit the end of the line. The winner is the one that gets there first."

He drew his pistol, aiming it in the air. "Good luck!" Tanner's pistol fired, and Astondo swung its mallet down, splintering the wooden tie with the spike. Hissing, Astondo continued to the next spike.

Wong closed his eyes and sat cross-legged on the track.

"Well," Coopersmith smiled, "it seems your man has fallen asleep on the job."

Tanner waved him off. "Don't worry. He always does this when he's fixing to raise a ruckus."

Wong let his mind drift away to an empty silent place. He let his breathing slow, and through the darkness of his thoughts came an image of the past.

Sunlight filtered between the blossoming branches of the temple's courtyard. Dressed in orange robes, Master Chew listened to skylarks' songs from the east. As Wong approached him, the old master presented him with a sword. With an outstretched hand, Master Chew directed him toward a wooden dummy dressed in an iron breastplate.

"Use the sword to cut the armor."

Gritting his teeth, Wong slashed at the armor, each strike sending a shock up his arm as the blade glanced off. He hacked until his arm grew slow and heavy.

"Enough," Master Chew said, taking back the sword. "The edge is too wide to pierce the armor. Wild reckless action only dulls it."

The master held out the sword, letting sunlight glint off the blade. "A sword's tip allows the weapon to direct the attack to a point."

Master Chew drove the tip of the sword through the armor.

"Where thoughtless broad attack fails, the focused attack cuts a path to victory." The master handed Wong the sword, and the image blasted into a brilliant light, swirling and spilling over with power.

Wong pushed the light into his stomach, allowing it to radiate through his body. He let the waves of energy wash over him until they became one steady pulse of power. Wong's eyes sprang open.

He flew into the air, hanging suspended over the workers. Leading with his hammer, Wong came down, driving the first spike straight through the tie.

Wong cartwheeled down the track. With every revolution his hammer blasted a spike into the timbers, picking up speed as he went.

Halfway down the track, the bronze machine continued systematically hammering spikes with mechanical efficiency. It stopped and stared as Wong spun past him, driving in the last three spikes on the track.

Behind them, the workers exploded into cheers. They mobbed Wong, applauding and thumping him on the back.

"Well, Coppersmith," Tanner grinned, "it looks like you owe me a hundred dollars."

Frowning, Coppersmith handed over a wad of folded bills.

Quivering, Astondo's eyes flared as the money changed hands.

Pointing to the bronze giant, Wong said, "Might be better than any man, maybe even better than any Chinaman, but not better than a railroad man," and plucked his winnings out of Tanner's grasp. With that, the other workers erupted into applause.

Steam blasted from Astondo's ears. It raised its mallet high into the air.

Coppersmith held up his hands. "Astondo! Stop!"

"Alright now," Tanner said, drawing his pistol. "Don't make another move."

The machine advanced as Tanner fired, bullets ricocheting off of its metal skin. Astondo swung down.

"Oh, horse-feathers," Tanner gulped.

Before the mallet stuck, Wong pushed the rail boss behind Coppersmith's wagon.

Through the dust, Coppersmith blocked the machine and held up his hands. "Halt, I say!"

Astondo flattened its inventor to the ground in a single strike. Around it, workers screamed, scattering in all directions. The metal monster lifted its mallet; gooey strands of Coppersmith dangled from the end.

Its head swiveled around, scanning the area. Screams caught the machine's attention and it stomped off, crashing past Coppersmith's wagon and over to the men's tents.

"Well, go on!" Tanner hollered at Wong. "Get him!"

"Forty-sixty."

"What? Why, you yellow bastard!"

Astondo kicked a horse over the train cars.

"And the rest of the day off for all the men," Wong said.

Tanner slapped two more fives in Wong's hand. "Fine."

Wong ran after Astondo as it smashed through the camp, scattering men and horses. It used its claw to overturn carts and its mallet to flatten any unlucky workers who came within striking distance.

Flipping into the air, Wong landed on the machine's shoulders. He found a handhold on the collar and held tight as the bronze monster tromped through screaming workers.

Wong slammed the ridge of his hand into Astondo's neck. It made an impressive clang, but hurt his hand more than the machine. Using its claw, Astondo plucked Wong from its back and flung him toward the ground.

Landing on his feet, Wong rolled away as Astondo roared out a spray of blistering steam that melted two cowering workers. With a yell, Wong flew at the giant, slamming its torso with his fists and feet. The metal monster glared at him with glowing amber eyes and casually swatted him away.

Wong crashed in the dirt. Blood trickled from his lips as his eyes rolled back to whites.

When he opened them again, Wong was holding Zhu Yan in his arms, her belly swollen like the harvest moon that floated above them.

"It's only a few years," Wong whispered. "Our actions must be focused, like the tip of a blade, so that we can carve a future for our family."

He kissed her head. "It's a small sacrifice."

Zhu Yan leaned back, her eyes wet. "You only have to close your eyes, and I will be with you."

The memory ended as Astondo knocked over a dynamite wagon, rocking the camp with a mushroom cloud of fire and smoke. Wong staggered to his feet and surveyed the demolished camp. "Tanner!"

From behind an overturned service car, the rail boss peeked out. "I thought you was squished into strawberry preserves!"

Wong picked up a discarded hammer. "Get some spikes," he said as he wiped blood from his face.

Together, they followed the path of destruction to the rear of the supply line, where they found Astondo flattening a horse and rider into the dust. They crouched behind a smoldering chuck wagon as the metal monster scanned the devastation.

Astondo turned and saw them. Steam whistling from its ears, it charged.

"Spike!" Wong shouted as he jumped high into the air.

Tanner flung the spike at Astondo. It tumbled toward the monster's face, end over end.

Twisting in the air, Wong reared back with the hammer. Just as the tip of the spike touched Astondo's forehead, Wong struck, driving the spike deep into the machine.

Sparks flashed as smoke drifted from the wound. With a groan, Astondo teetered and slammed to the ground.

It twitched, then lay still as the light faded from its eyes.

Wong Heng Li gathered his things while the men celebrated. Shrugging off their cheers, he returned to his spot in the spring sun and lowered his hat over his eyes.

Soon, he was dreaming of home.

Frank Larnerd is an undergraduate student at WVSU, where he received multiple awards for fiction and non-fiction. His first anthology as editor, "Hills of Fire: Bare-Knuckle Yarns of Appalachia" will be released in the fall of 2012 from Woodland Press. He lives in Putnam County, West Virginia.

Flying Devils

Derwin Mak

Soong Kanghua walked along the shoreline of Kunming Lake in the grounds of the Summer Palace. Servants and officials bowed to him as he passed. He was the Assistant Minister of Finance in the Ministry of War.

He approached the Marble Boat. He disliked the pavilion, which was shaped like a European paddle steamer. The Imperial Family had built it with funds meant for the construction of a modern navy. Soong was powerless to stop the embezzlement. Like many things of the Qing Dynasty, it was beautiful but useless.

The Minister of War awaited him in the Marble Boat. Soong bowed to the Minister, a general of the first rank.

"Your Excellency, what may I do for you?" Soong asked.

"I wish you to investigate some rumors about General Zhou Desheng," the Minister said. "Do you know him?"

"Not well," Soong replied. "I know that he commands several forts in Guangxi Province, and he watches the French on the Vietnam side of the border. Has he been a problem?"

"I have heard that he is levying an unauthorized tax on the local population. Investigate this allegation. Examine his accounting records to determine the source of his funds."

Yet another warlord is extorting money from the locals, Soong thought. Why treat this one differently?

The Minister handed a scroll to Soong. "This is my authorization for you to execute Zhou if you find any evidence of wrongdoing. No trial is required."

The latest power struggle among generals, Soong realized.

"If you need to execute him, you will receive ten thousand yuan to compensate you for the inconvenience," the Minister added.

"Your Excellency is most kind."

"One hundred Manchu Bannermen will escort you. Zhou keeps only fifty men at his headquarters, so you will outnumber him two to one."

Soong looked at the scroll. "Your Excellency, if there is a possibility that Zhou will need, uh, military discipline, why send me instead of a military officer to investigate him?"

"I cannot spare any competent officer on this mission," the Minister said. "I need them all to concentrate on strengthening the military."

After China's shameful loss to Japan, the Minister needed to show some commitment to the Self-Strengthening Movement. Sending a general to kill another general would be awkward at this time. An accountant would be a better assassin.

Soong bowed. "I understand, sir. Thank you for entrusting me with this important mission."

As Soong left the Summer Palace, he watched some riflemen at target practice. They fired at a bulls-eye mounted in a rowboat in Kunming Lake. Nobody hit the target. Their officer, a low-ranking prince, simply shrugged.

Chinese soldiers were useless. Unlike in the West, soldiering was a despised occupation if one was below the rank of general. Chinese soldiers did not show off their uniforms and medals to parents and girlfriends. Chinese men joined the army only for food and clothes. They gave their feeble loyalty to individual generals, not to their country.

As a wealthy official, Soong lived in a large *siheyuan*. It was a traditional home, a walled compound with four buildings surrounding a courtyard. It was also the local office of the Hung League, named after the first Ming Emperor.

Soong watched his thirty warriors in training. A *Shaolin* monk taught hand-to-hand combat to new recruits. In another corner, some men fought with *dao* swords. At a long table, the riflemen cleaned their guns. A color party carried a banner reading, "Down with the Qing and up with the Ming!"

Training a secret society was dangerous in Beijing, a city full of soldiers and civil servants. Fortunately, Soong's high rank and loyal service kept him from suspicion. Nobody had questioned the thousands of yuan that he had recorded as office supplies in the Ministry's accounting records. The money actually went to feed, equip, and clothe the Hung League.

Soong called for attention. The men quietly gathered around him.

"Some of you wonder what chance we have of defeating the foreign devils when the Imperial Army has failed," Soong began. "Know that the Army has been corrupted by the Qing, a dynasty of weak Manchus. But we, through our martial and spiritual training, embody the true Han spirit. We are the heroes of *The Water Margin*. We are the *wuxia*. We will defeat the foreign devils."

When Soong arrived at General Zhou's fort, he told the Bannermen to stay outside the walls.

"Sir, should we not enter the fort?" asked Captain Arsai, the Bannermen's commander.

"No. I want to settle things peacefully," Soong explained.

At the fort's gate, Zhou's sentries eyed the Bannermen warily. Zhou's sentries and Soong's Bannermen were all Chinese soldiers, but they came from different worlds. The Bannermen wore Manchu-style blue shirts and baggy pants, with Mandarin hats for the officers and turbans for the lower ranks. Some carried swords and bows and arrows, and others carried rifles. In contrast, Zhou's soldiers wore khaki European military tunics and peaked caps. Each carried a rifle.

The sentries opened the gate, and Soong entered the fort, unarmed and alone.

The fort was small, just slightly larger than Soong's home in Beijing. Zhou had built the fort by adding four watch towers and additional masonry to an existing *siheyuan*. He had also built a gate in the wall that faced a lake, thus creating an opening to the shore.

General Zhou greeted his visitor. "Assistant Minister Soong, welcome to my headquarters. Will you join me for tea?"

"Yes, that would be nice," Soong replied. They walked through the back gate and sat at a table by the shore.

"This is a beautiful lake, is it not?" Zhou said. "It is so quiet and peaceful."

Someone yelled profanities and, "Release me! Release me! You cannot keep me here!"

Soong saw a junk floating on the lake. A man was tied to its mast.

"Who is that?" Soong asked.

Zhou sipped his tea. "He is a worthless opium dealer whom I have arrested. That boat is his private yacht. It is pretty, is it not? It is unfortunate that it will be used in target practice."

"Why did you arrest him? What target practice?"

Zhou did not answer the questions. "Like I said, this is a quiet and peaceful lake."

Soong looked at the books lying on the table. In addition to Sun Tzu's *The Art of War*, there was a Chinese translation of Carl von Clausewitz's *On War*. The General also had a book called *Robur the Conqueror* by the French author Jules Verne.

"I see that you like foreign ideas," Soong said.

"Foreign ideas are our best weapon against the foreigners," said Zhou.

"That is why the military has the Self-Strengthening Movement."

"Those funds were spent on a boat made of stone."

"I had nothing to do with that," Soong said.

General Zhou nodded and sipped his tea.

Soong broke the silence. "There is a rumor among the local people. Some of them have alleged that you have been charging a tax on them. Is that true?"

"Yes it is," Zhou admitted without hesitating. His brazenness surprised Soong.

"For what purpose?"

"To develop modern weapons."

"But you already get funding to buy new weapons."

"Money from the Self-Strengthening Movement is not enough. I need money to *develop* modern weapons, not just buy guns from Europe."

"Perhaps he will understand when he sees our invention," said a voice from behind. Soong turned and saw a European walking to them. The man wore a white blazer and black pants, looking like a foreign trader in Shanghai.

General Zhou stood. "Allow me to introduce Monsieur Albert Tissandier. He is an architect and aviator. He piloted a balloon out of Paris during the German siege of the city. He received a bravery medal for that mission."

"The General flatters me," Tissandier said as he shook Soong's hand. "It is an honor to meet you, Assistant Minister. Please excuse my poor ability to speak Chinese."

"Join us for tea," Zhou said.

As Soong sipped his tea, he noticed that no walls or barricades blocked off the land between the fort and the lake. Anyone could approach the fort's rear from the lakeshore.

Soong heard a dull roar in the sky. In the distance, a cylindrical object appeared above the trees.

"Is that a balloon?" Soong asked. The object's speed amazed him.

"It is similar but not the same. It is an airship."

The airship flew closer and closer until it hovered over the shore. Its cylindrical envelope was tapered at both ends. Men peered down from a long gondola underneath the envelope. Smoke and steam rose from machinery behind the gondola. The flag of Imperial China fluttered from a mast.

Zhou explained how his airship flew. It was made of white canvas stretched over a metal framework; hence, the framework maintained the envelope's shape. The envelope was full of hydrogen, a buoyant but flammable gas. Six men worked in the gondola. Behind the gondola, an elaborate steam engine drove the propellers. To protect the hydrogen from the heat and fire of the engine, a sheet of asbestos-coated steel protected the lower half of the envelope.

"It is the most advanced powered balloon in the world," Zhou boasted."

"Remarkable," Soong said. "Who designed it?"

"I conceived of the idea and instructed Monsieur Tissandier to design it," Zhou said. He motioned to the Tissandier, who smiled at Soong.

Zhou continued. "I built the airship with local labor and materials. The engine and weaponry came from France, but otherwise, the airship was built by Chinese."

"Your workers learn quickly," said Tissandier. "Your country has great industrial potential if its workers are trained and led properly."

The opium dealer on the junk yelled again. "Untie me! Let me go!"

Zhou put down his cup of tea. "It is time for the target practice."

He stood up, waved at the airship's crew, and pointed at the lake.

The airship flew over the junk. Suddenly, machine gun fire erupted from the gondola. The opium dealer shrieked before the bullets tore through his chest.

Tissandier grinned and said, "Hotchkiss machine gun, the best in France."

Next, four bombs dropped from the airship onto the junk. The boat burst into flames and sank.

"Congratulations, General, another successful test," Tissandier said.

Zhou smiled. The airship turned and descended on the land.

"The Ministry of War did not authorize the construction of this machine," said Soong.

"Do you not see its potential?" Zhou said. "Attack the enemy from the air! Sink their ships before they can carry their soldiers to our shores. In the future, who controls the air will control the land and the sea."

Soong guffawed. "All you have done is sink one unarmed junk with one defenseless man aboard."

"I have just one airship, but think how a fleet of them will stand up against the enemy gunboats."

"It is a brilliant idea," Tissandier agreed.

Soong turned to Tissandier. "If this idea is so brilliant, why have the French not used it?"

"My government is not as forward-looking as General Zhou," Tissandier said. "Fortunately, it has no restrictions against my selling my expertise to friendly foreign states. Your Excellency, with a fleet of airships, China will rule Asia again. Just stay out of Indo-China."

"Do not worry, you can keep Vietnam," Soong said ruefully.

Zhou pointed at the airship. "This is what we need to expel the foreign devils and make China strong again."

Soong shook his head. "We have bought foreign guns and made ironclad ships. Still, we keep losing. Imitating the Westerners is not working."

"Then how do you suggest we fight back?" Zhou demanded.

"Go back to an old tradition," Soong said. "Train thousands of men in Chinese martial arts. Instill national pride in them. Revive the *wuxia*."

"We can do that with Western weapons," Zhou insisted. "Our problem is not the weapons. Our problem is that we use modern weapons with ancient tactics. If we adopt Western military science, we can win a war. Look at what the Japanese have achieved."

"I hate the Japanese," Soong said.

The airship's crew marched towards them, halted, and saluted. General Zhou returned the salute.

"May I inspect the troops?" Soong asked.

Zhou nodded. Soong went to the first airman and asked, "How did you learn to fly the airship?"

"I spent a year in France learning aeronautics from Monsieur Tissandier," the man replied.

"Interesting. Have you received any training in hand-to-hand combat, sword fighting, or rifle shooting?"

"I received training on how to operate a machine gun."

This man hides behind equipment and fears close combat with the enemy, Soong thought.

"General, I need to talk to you in private," he said. "Please dismiss your men and the foreigner."

Zhou ordered Tissandier and the airmen to go into the fort. Now only Zhou and Soong stood at the shore.

"General, thank you for demonstrating your airship," Soong said. "However, I cannot endorse the construction of such machines."

Zhou frowned. "I guess that is why you brought one hundred Bannermen."

"As a financial official, I must stop unauthorized taxes and expenditures. It is my duty."

"Hah! Your duty is to protect the corrupt Qing."

"No, my duty is to protect our country from the foreign devils," Soong protested. "That should be your duty too. Instead, you are becoming like them."

"I am not the foreign devil," Zhou said. "The Qing are the foreign devils."

Soong paused. Then he whispered, "Down with the Qing and up with the Ming."

Zhou smiled and nodded.

"Then join us," Soong said. "All over China, martial arts masters are training warriors who will rise up against the foreign devils. The revival of *wuxia* is the only way. Join us."

Zhou shook his head. "As romantic as *wuxia* are, I prefer modern weapons and tactics."

"We are at an impasse," Soong observed sadly. "General, I must return to Beijing now."

Zhou escorted Soong back into the fort and to the front gate. They bowed to each other, and Soong walked out. The gate slammed shut behind him.

Captain Arsai asked, "Sir, do you want us to storm the fort?"

"That will not be necessary," Soong said. "General Zhou has a strange balloon. It lies on a lakeshore behind the fort. The shore is not fortified, so we can go around the fort and destroy the balloon."

"What if General Zhou wants to oppose us?"

"Then he and his men will leave the fort and engage us on the lakeshore, where we will outnumber him two to one."

"A good plan, sir," Arsai said.

"Give me a sword," Soong said. "I will lead the attack with you."

Arsai looked shocked. He probably had not expected a civilian official to want to fight.

"Captain, give me a sword," Soong demanded again. Arsai ordered his men to bring a *dao* to Soong.

The Bannermen split into two groups, one led by Arsai, the other by Soong. They encircled the fort as they ran towards the rear. Zhou's soldiers fired rifles from the watchtowers. A few Bannermen fell to the bullets. Soong raised his sword and yelled at his men to keep running.

The two groups met at the shore. The airship sat moored to the ground.

"That is the balloon!" Soong shouted, pointing his sword at the airship. "Riflemen, shoot at it!"

The riflemen aimed and fired. Their bullets bounced harmlessly off the airship.

Soong grunted. The riflemen had shot at the steel-protected part of the airship's envelope.

"Aim higher!" he urged. "Aim for the top half of the balloon."

The fort's rear gate opened. Zhou's men charged out with bayonets fixed on their rifles. War cries filled the air. When Zhou's men opened fire, the Bannermen shot back.

"Keep firing at the balloon!" Soong yelled.

Arsai pointed at two riflemen. "Keep shooting at the airship!" he ordered. "We will cover you."

But before the two riflemen could pierce the airship, Zhou's soldiers swarmed them. One got shot in the chest, and the other got stabbed by a bayonet.

Hand-to-hand fighting broke out. Bayonets clashed against swords and arrows and bullets flew through the air.

Soong saw General Zhou, Tissandier, and some officers standing at the gate. Like all generals, Zhou did not lead his troops into combat, but rather, directed the battle from the rear.

Armed only with a sword, Soong ran through the fighting, towards the gate. One of Zhou's officers aimed a pistol at him, but the General raised his hand, and the officer lowered his gun.

When Soong stopped in front of Zhou, the General unsheathed his sword. It was not a traditional Chinese sword like Soong's *dao*. Instead, it had a Japanese-style blade with a European hilt. Officers of the modernized armies carried such swords, a sign of their foreign training.

"General, are you surrendering?" Soong asked, looking at the sword.

"No, you are!" Zhou cried as he lunged at Soong.

Soong darted backwards and hit his *dao* against Zhou's sword. The clash of steel upon steel filled the air.

Zhou's officers raised their pistols. He yelled, "Lower your guns! I will take him down!"

"Join me!" Soong urged as they fought.

"No!"

"Would you rather be a flying devil or a *wuxia*?"

"I will be *China's* flying devil!"

They lunged at each other, parrying each other's thrusts, and passing backwards and forwards. Soong, who had trained with the best swordsmen in Beijing, could not defeat Zhou. The General, despite his Western ideas, fought like a *wuxia*.

Suddenly, an explosion rocked the shore. Soong saw the airship burst into a ball of flame. A rifleman must have pierced the envelope and ignited the hydrogen.

Stunned by the blast and heat, Zhou froze and stared at his burning airship. Soong lowered his sword and watched with him.

Though Soong and Zhou had stopped fighting, the battle continued. Bullets flew past them.

Zhou groaned and fell to the ground. Blood poured from a bullet wound in his chest.

Soong dropped his sword and knelt beside Zhou. The general grabbed Soong's shoulder and whispered, "Down with the Qing and up with the Ming."

Zhou coughed up blood, convulsed, and lay still.

An officer walked to Soong and pointed a revolver at him.

"I am Captain Li. I command the fort now," said the officer. "Your Excellency, hold up your hands."

Soong stood up but did not raise his hands. Li glared at him.

Li said to Tissandier, "You must leave immediately. Wait by the front gate. My men will escort you to the Vietnam border."

"*Merci beaucoup*," Tissandier blurted as he retreated into the fort.

Li turned to Soong. "You will tell your men to stand down, and I will do likewise. Then we will negotiate a truce. Do you agree?"

Soong nodded silently as he watched the airship burn.

"I thank you most profusely for solving this problem," said the Minister of War.

"It was my duty," said Soong.

"What was Zhou doing with the money that he extorted from the peasants?"

"He wasted it on gambling, opium, and other vices," Soong lied. He had not told anyone about the airship.

"That is so sad. Fortunately, Captain Li — excuse me, General Li — will be a much better commander."

The Minister handed an envelope to Soong. "Please accept this as compensation for the inconvenience that General Zhou caused you."

Soong took the envelope and bowed. "Thank you, Your Excellency. I remain loyal and at your service."

He used the ten thousand yuan to buy more swords and rifles for the Hung League.

Four years later, Soong received a visitor from the Society of Righteous and Harmonious Fists. The Righteous and Harmonious Fists was much larger than the Hung League. The foreign devils called them "Boxers," referring to a combat sport.

"We are seeking the aid of all martial societies, big and small," the Boxer said. "Together, we will expel the foreign devils."

Although the Boxers declared loyalty to the Qing, their plan tempted Soong. The Han could always overthrow the Qing after expelling the foreigners.

"We will be your allies," Soong said. "Destroy the foreigners."

In 1899, the Righteous and Harmonious Fists rose up to kill the foreign devils. The counterattack was an orgy of killing, raping and looting. It was China's greatest humiliation.

Soong died in combat in Beijing. He and his warriors charged into battle with swords and rifles. The Japanese Marines returned fire with machine guns.

In Tokyo, Admiral Togo received documents that his Marines had looted from the home of Soong Kanghua, an official of the Chinese Ministry of War.

Togo looked at the plans for a steam-powered balloon, along with drawings of the balloon dropping bombs on ships.

How interesting, the Admiral thought.

On December 8, 1941, Tokyo Time, Japanese airplanes sank five battleships and wrecked three destroyers at the U.S. Navy base in Pearl Harbor, Hawaii.

The flying devils had come.

Derwin Mak's story "Transubstantiation" won the 2006 Aurora Award for Best Short Form Work in English. He co-edited, with Eric Choi, *The Dragon and the Stars*, the first anthology of science fiction and fantasy by overseas Chinese, which won the 2011 Aurora Award for Best Related Work in English. He has also written about East Asian pop culture and anime for magazines.

Legend of the Secret Masterpiece

Nick Tramdack

The airboat ascended through the city shaft, skirting cliff-bazaars and sculpture gardens, gaining the airspace over rickety wooden patios. Sustained by the liftglaze painted on its wooden hull, it soared obliquely over a buttressed bridge. Lights fell past the hull like flowers: paper lanterns in cadmium yellow and stageblood red, sawdust torches in the bitter distance.

Rainer set his chin on his palm and stared over the gunwale. Wind spoiled the boy's ponytail, checked at the pink bandanna around his neck. His flannel jacket and canvas shorts couldn't block the chill: goose bumps rose on his hands and skinny legs.

The airboat nestled up to a wooden dock cantilevered into the void. Naphtha lanterns lined the thoroughfare beyond it. Under that light a street mapmaker was scrawling one-offs for pedestrians.

The boatman prodded Rainer with a sandaled foot. "You want higher, kid, you gotta pay."

"The heroes always hook rides across the Shaft of Treasons," Rainer said. "Can't you let me ride along?"

The boatman spat. "Pick up your johns at the Hot-Liver, not in my taxi!"

In fact, Rainer had used this strategy to get customers before. But tonight he was just angling for a free ride to the coin locker in Serapion Square where he'd stashed his warm jacket and some lemon drops and lambskins and a chocolate bar and a dagger. Rainer had just one coin left and he needed it to open that locker.

"I can't work the Hot-Liver anymore," Rainer said.

"Yeah, well, we all got problems. Now scram!"

"Ahoy there!" a voice boomed from the dock. "Goin' up?"

Rainer turned. The old man's body looked like a pumpkin set atop a stepstool and enfolded in blue robes. His hair was gray and close and he wore half a dozen gold rings in each ear. Wrinkles and scars marbled his deep brown skin like mahogany. A ceramic wine-jug was clipped onto his empty swordbelt with a carabiner. *Typical washed-up hero,* Rainer thought.

"There's a weight limit, friend," said the boatman. "And this kid won't—"

"I'm in a hurry!"

Before the boatman could protest, the fat hero hopped into the airboat. But the craft only sank a few inches — for a guy that large, Rainer would've expected a foot at least.

"Which way ya headed, little brother?"

"Serapion Square."

The hero nodded to the boatman. "You heard the fellow! Up!"

"It'll be triple fare," said the boatman.

"Why? This boat ain't overweight!"

"It looks it, though! If the Guild spots us, they'll fine me thirty K!"

Maybe next time, kid. It's my ride, so clear out. That's what Rainer expected to hear from the fat hero.

Instead, the hero tossed the boatman a thirty-K coin.

The boatman caught it down-hand, flashed a toadyish grin, and the airboat ascended. The fat man took a swig of wine. Rainer huddled in his jacket and continued looking over the gunwale.

Below them was another airboat — a taxi, gaining altitude. It was following their course.

"Take that shaft on the left," said the fat man.

"Serapion's not that way."

"Do it."

The boatman banked the airboat into the shaft. It rose, spiraling around its center of gravity like a leaf in a stream. Lights descended. Rainer looked down again. The second airboat followed them. There were two men on board: the pilot, and a figure in white robes, a sword slung across his back.

"*Stop!*"

The voice rose up the shaft like iron dropped on stone.

"That's a hero down there!" Rainer cried.

"Aw, shit," said the boatman. "You got me *tailed*?"

Words echoed upward: *"You can't run, Gil-Martin!"*

"Put on some steam!" the fat man ordered.

"This ain't no getaway craft!"

Rainer swallowed. Rivalry, challenge, revenge — he didn't care about martial world intrigues, but this rickety airboat hovered over a one-minute drop. And in Nocturne City, heroes rarely stopped to consider collateral damage. Besides, the corpulent, weaponless Gil-Martin looked ... well...

"Oh, this is just great!" Rainer squeaked. "They're about to sink us, and you don't even have a sword!"

Gil-Martin uncorked his jug and took a three-second swig.

"This Rose Thorn Wine is truly exquisite," he murmured, wiping his mouth with a grimy sleeve. "Since it's the last jug left in Nocturne City, I was happy to make — a certain trade..."

Rainer gaped. "You traded your sword for a *bottle of wine?*"

"Swords only cause problems," twinkled Gil-Martin. "But wine can make problems go away. That's why trading is always the optimal move."

"He's gaining fast!" the boatman wailed. "We're too heavy!"

"I'll shed some ballast," said Gil-Martin, rising to his feet. He fumbled in his robes and began to piss over the gunwale. "Ho ho, look at it rain — oop!"

Gil-Martin's off-hand swept out into the void.

Silver flashed.

His hand returned — now pinching a six-inch silver needle between two fingers. Grimacing, the hero tossed it into space.

"Don't look down," he ordered, while Rainer scooted onto the center bench. "Boatman! When we hit the top of this shaft, hard starboard and—"

"Gil-Martiiiin!"

Gil-Martin froze, then tore the robe back from his forearm. Rainer did the same. His gooseflesh was rippling.

"Impossible," whispered Gil-Martin. "Five—"

He shoved Rainer forward.

From the bottom of the boat, Rainer saw Gil-Martin leap upwards.

While his fat body hung preposterously in the air, a plane of purple light bisected the airboat on a line from bow to stern, just missing the place Rainer had been.

Gil-Martin landed right behind Rainer — which should have overturned the hull, but didn't.

Because the airboat had been split into two equal halves.

Eyes wide, mouth open, every hair on his body standing up, Rainer watched the boatman tumble into the fissure. The body came apart on the way down.

Rainer screeched, grappling for purchase. His left hand gripped the seam where the boat had been sliced; his right, the starboard gunwale. Somehow he and Gil-Martin brought the halved hull into a tricky balance.

But the liftglaze on its bottom couldn't keep the busted hull aloft. It sank. It spun, a hundred feet from any wall. Markets, walkways, torchlit fryshops passed from down to up.

They spiraled past the other airboat. Rainer saw the hero standing aboard it. His windblown hair, beard, robes, desiccated face, were whiter than milk.

The white-clad ghoul leapt off his airboat, straight toward Rainer and Gil-Martin.

But Rainer's hull-half was falling slower now — because Gil-Martin had already left it.

Rainer looked up—

To see the two rivals, thin and fat, white and dark, collide in midair.

Gil-Martin got first footing. He *punted* the other hero into the abyss, backflipping off his kick.

The white shape fell away without a sound.

Gently as a cat, Gil-Martin landed behind Rainer again.

They steered the hull down-right, missing a metal line by inches as they landed it atop a descending cablecar.

The boy collapsed onto the seven-foot-square roof. Gil-Martin kicked the hull away and settled next to him and took a long drink. He offered Rainer the jug.

"Go on, little brother!"

Shivering, he took a swig. It really was good wine — it hadn't been cut with anything, that was how Rainer knew.

"At least he's gone," Rainer said. "Nobody could survive that fall."

"No. White Revenant will."

"How? What *is* that guy?"

"He's not … really human anymore. Even if he falls into hell itself, he'll climb up after me." The skin around Gil-Martin's eyes tightened. "In the last ten years, he's done it countless times."

"What was that attack? That liftglaze should've stopped an axe!"

Gil-Martin sighed.

"Supreme martial arts, little brother. A technique that strikes its target's true essence, rather than its vulgar shadow in the material world. The ultimate evil style: Five Space-Time Vortex!"

"Can you beat it?"

"No. Nobody can. Its only weakness is that it can't be used twice in a row — otherwise, we'd both be dead right now!"

The cablecar clicked downwards into a cutaway through solid rock. The half-light grew chill; damp fog veiled the distance. Rainer hugged his knees, shivering.

'Snow' began falling upwards through the haze — ash particles, miasma vented from forges and foundries miles below. Rainer pulled a face.

"What's wrong?"

"It stinks!"

"Does it?" Gil-Martin smiled. "I can't smell anything. White Revenant once tried to kill me with poison gas. Luckily I spotted a discolored copper coin in time and ran — but I lost my sense of smell forever. That's why now, I only drink the strongest wine!"

Rainer grinned back shyly and took another gulp.

"How old are you, little brother? What's your name?"

"I'm Rainer — and I'm old enough to drink wine!"

Gil-Martin just stared into the ascending snow around them.

"What're you going to do?"

"A long time ago," Gil-Martin said, "there was this bum — a street mapmaker. A real master. His maps were so beautiful, people'd commission 'em for places they'd never even go... But one day ... no, everyone says 'one night' in this town ... one night he sold everything he had and became a bum again. He said he was gonna wander 'til he learned to draw a final map. A *perfect* map. A map to the heart of the city."

"And?"

"He vanished! But people started thinking," Gil-Martin added slyly, "If that map existed, what would it lead to?"

"Maybe ... a treasure?"

"Or a weapon. Or a place to hide, somewhere White Revenant couldn't find me. That's why for ten years, I've been chasin' that bum's secret masterpiece, and White Revenant's been chasin' me. But I never had any luck at all — until tonight."

Smiling, Gil-Martin produced an envelope from his robes and unfolded it.

Rainer whistled. The gorgeous map must've come to ten thousand pen-strokes. It was Nocturne City, from the earth's surface down to the lava flows beneath the foundries. Every line was see-through, yet definite. In one corner was a red seal, a sideways figure-eight.

But Gil-Martin slumped forward and closed his eyes.

"Maximalist … blunt … vulgar. It's a fake!"

More 'snow' ascended.

"Hey," Rainer finally whispered. "Don't be sad, old man."

"Why shouldn't I be?"

"Well…" Rainer's face felt hot. "'Cause you're terrific, that's why. You've got tons of skills. But me, I've got no skills at all. The only way I can make a K is selling my body."

"That's not true. You helped me steer that airboat down. That means you can think fast. You saw something horrible, but you pulled it together. That proves you're brave. Better yet, you've drunk wine with me, which means you're my friend now." Gil-Martin smiled. "And in this world, being a friend isn't a skill possessed by everyone."

Rainer looked away and laughed the ironic laugh he used whenever something threatened to stir his heart.

"Anyway, I've got a job in mind for you, little brother."

"What, a blowjob?"

"Not that kind of job," said Gil-Martin. "If this map's a fake, there's only one person who could've made the switch. I need someone to get inside his houseboat. I can't do it without raising an alarm. But a little guy like you…"

"What's the payout?"

"An even split," said Gil-Martin. "Half the treasure. If there's no treasure, half the map's value as an art object."

"And if it's another fake?"

"A shot at ten thousand K."

Ten thousand K was more than Rainer would earn in two years on the street.

"It's a deal!"

Rainer expected Gil-Martin to smile back at him, but the big hero just muttered:

"If you knew the houseboat I meant, I wonder if you'd agree so fast!"

Every week, Baron d'Urtal chose a girl.

The volunteers gathered in the vestibule of his two-hundred-foot houseboat. They received unsigned money orders for 10,000 Kronzer and made them out to whomever they pleased. Then d'Urtal would emerge and examine the candidates one by one. As he dismissed each girl, he'd take back her money order.

When just one girl remained, d'Urtal would sign her paper, seal it and send it off by courier.

The houseboat would then cast off and float over to the Shaft of Vermillion Transcendence.

After an hour or two, it would float back home again.

Except, perhaps, for the top-flight heroes on his payrolls, nobody knew what d'Urtal did to the girls before he threw them into the shaft.

But Nocturne City was Nocturne City. The Baron's vestibule had never once gone empty.

Tonight, the vestibule held four young women and Rainer.

Silent, they sat on straight-backed chairs opposite a refreshment table. One girl nibbled numbly on a cordialed pear. Another nursed a flute of white wine. A thirtyish hero in white stockings and scale armor lounged against wainscoting, smoking a cigarette and watching himself in a gold-framed mirror. His left hand never moved from his longsword's tasseled hilt.

Rainer was terrified, yet somehow proud. It wasn't like he had any beard yet, and the clothes and cosmetics applied by Gil-Martin had gone a long way. The old man had even pinched pressure points on Rainer's lower back, shoulders, and inner thighs, to make him walk in a more feminine manner. Rainer thought he made quite a pretty girl indeed.

If this job falls apart, and I survive, maybe I could use this gimmick on the street.

There was just one problem — the girl next to him was even prettier. Her hair was also styled into a chignon, but hers had a superior sheen. Her skin was fairer, her nose smaller, and her ears didn't stick out so far. Her throat also lacked an "apple of knowledge." Rainer had tried to hide his own under a white ribbon. His palms were sweating, moistening the money order in his hand.

"Hey," he whispered. "He'll pick you, I know it!"

"Stop it." Her whisper was far higher than his. "You're making it worse!"

"Walk out right now," Rainer whispered, "and I'll sign my money order over to you."

The girl was silent.

"I'll prove it. Tell me your name."

"Icelina," she whispered. "Longchamp Rungs, three-two."

Rainer started to get up.

"Don't make it out to me!" She tugged at Rainer's dress. "To my father — Jules Wandreth, Longchamp Rungs, 32."

Keeping perfect posture, Rainer rose, went across to the table with the inkwell, and made out the order to Icelina Wandreth's father.

He felt sick. Not about the ten thousand K he was signing away in the hope the map was genuine — the number still seemed unreal to him — but about Icelina, still faithful to the father who had ordered her to sell herself. Rainer had always told himself that if only he had parents things would be different. But maybe Nocturne City could break anything, no matter how well it began.

He took his seat and flashed Icelina the paper.

The girl's tears glowed in the candlelight. "Why are you doing this?"

Rainer said nothing. Icelina wiped her eyes and got up and walked past the hero on guard. She cleared the door and ran down the gangplank.

"There's always one..." The hero threw his cigarette into a potted plum. "Well ladies, any other walk-outs? No? Then we'll begin."

The door to Rainer's left opened. He didn't dare look up. Black slippers with red pompoms strolled into his view, then out again.

D'Urtal stood before the first candidate, his baritone voice dripping refinement. "I fancy I have seen your face before, madame."

A money order changed hands with a crinkle. Footsteps trod carpet.

"I must decline tonight, my dear."

A wine flute clinked on a tray. The second girl stumbled out.

"Ah, you must favor me with your presence another time."

D'Urtal was speaking to the third girl, but looking straight at Rainer. Chills shook his spine as the girl handed d'Urtal her paper and left.

"If you would stand up, my little bird?"

Rainer obeyed. The Baron placed a cold forefinger under Rainer's chin and tilted it up. D'Urtal's face was long and clean-shaven and his breath smelled like rotten mulberries.

"Exquisite."

D'Urtal signed the money order to Jules Wandreth and handed it to the hero, who saluted, spun on a heel, and left. Rainer and d'Urtal were alone.

"I insist that you submit to a search," the Baron said. "I will retire; when my agent is finished, do proceed inward." He grinned, revealing a gold canine tooth. "But do not keep me waiting."

The Baron left. Rainer breathed again.

He reached beneath his skirt and removed from his stocking the glass vial Gil-Martin had given him. He peeled back the carpet and crushed the vial on the wood floor. When he was sure the fumes had spread, he rolled the carpet back over the shards. Then he returned to the chair, holding his hands modestly in his lap.

A stooped old woman in black entered from d'Urtal's door.

"Oh, madam," Rainer squeaked. "I can't, I'm so scared…"

"Ah, missy, there's nothing to fear—"

The old woman raised a hand to her eyes.

"Dear," she said, and collapsed to the carpet.

Rainer grinned. He reached into his skirt and palmed the other vial of poison. He'd taken the antidote a few hours earlier.

The room shifted under his feet. The houseboat had cast off.

Rainer fixed his hair before the mirror, pouted seductively, and crossed his fingers. He opened the door and passed through a corridor hung with a tapestry of devils dancing around a fire and put his hand on the knob to d'Urtal's suite.

He pushed the door inward. His eyes scanned the suite — red bedspread, curtained windows, desk, rugs. D'Urtal appeared in view. Rainer spotted a patch of bare floor. He threw the vial.

And, nimble as a dancer, d'Urtal intercepted the vial with his soft black pompomed slipper.

It didn't break.

"Silly little bird," whispered the Baron.

Rainer stumbled back, but his dress confused his movements.

D'Urtal's long cold fingers struck a pressure point below Rainer's white-ribboned throat. The blow hit him like a ball-peen hammer.

Rainer sat down — with a slam. He couldn't move. He could breathe and move his eyes, but flexing other muscles led to an instant cramp.

"Almost perfectly done." D'Urtal set the vial on the desk. "But your scent wasn't quite accurate."

Rainer strained. *Of course — the smell, the one detail Gil-Martin couldn't have checked!*

"You're not quite pretty enough for me to forget you're a boy," said d'Urtal. "But I've got another use for you…"

Fuck you, Rainer tried to say. It came out *hur hur.* He thought, *I only need to hold out a few more minutes—*

D'Urtal snapped his fingers. The four curtained windows in the suite burst open on their hinges. The ceiling lamp guttered in the cold air. A figure in pristine white robes walked soundlessly into the room, a sword slung across his back. It was White Revenant.

"This is Gil-Martin's little friend?" d'Urtal asked him.

"Yes, the boy's aura is definitely the same."

D'Urtal smiled. "The map's on the wall as you requested."

Without moving his head, White Revenant glanced to the side. Framed above the desk was a white paper. Like the fake map Gil-Martin had examined, a red figure-eight adorned one corner.

Except this map was made with just two pen strokes — two circles, one inside the other. They weren't accurate, or even concentric. They bulged. The artist's hand had wavered.

How could *this* be the map to the heart of the city?

"Hm," said White Revenant. "Just the scribbling of a senile old fool."

"This next bit should be quite entertaining," said d'Urtal, pouring himself a glass of red. "That butterball's martial arts are said to be quite extraordinary. I can hardly wait to see what happens next."

Rainer's eyes stung with tears and makeup. Not only was the map worthless, he'd become the bait d'Urtal and White Revenant had set for Gil-Martin!

Chuckling, d'Urtal lifted the glass to his lips.

And held it there without drinking.

A long thin silver needle had embedded itself in his throat.

White Revenant's hand returned to his side. He studied d'Urtal. The wine in the glass was moving due to the bobbing of the houseboat, but the dead Baron was frozen still.

"You talk too much, d'Urtal," said White Revenant.

Rainer squirmed. *If only I hadn't tried to bum a ride back there … if only I hadn't trusted Gil-Martin…*

White Revenant walked outside, onto a semicircular balcony with an ivory rail like a jaw's lower half. He waited. Beyond his white form, the Shaft of Vermillion Transcendence sank in profound gloom. Vagrant ash-flecks rose.

White Revenant returned to the suite and stood behind a wooden armoire so that someone on the balcony couldn't see him. He reached behind his shoulder and drew a sword. A frayed green tassel dangled sloppily from the pommel of its antique grip.

Rainer strained. Everybody knew that heroes could unblock their pressure points by exerting inner strength. This technique was akin to the lightness skills Gil-Martin had used to reduce his "weight" on the airboat taxi. But Rainer was just a whore. He didn't think *he* had any inner strength. Every muscle he moved tightened a barbed wire around his heart.

Without warning, Gil-Martin's enormous silhouette dropped onto the balcony.

Rainer understood that from Gil-Martin's perspective, the standing d'Urtal, the map, and Rainer would form a triangle, making White Revenant invisible.

The overweight hero stepped inside. White Revenant emerged from behind the armoire.

"Gil-Martin, you've finally appeared!"

"White Revenant!"

"The map on that wall is the bum's masterpiece. But I've got your sword, Eight Divine Harmonies — and it's pointed at your little friend."

Rainer swallowed. *That's the sword Gil-Martin sold before!*

"I owe you, Gil-Martin," said White Revenant. "The truth is, if you weren't my enemy, I wouldn't have mastered Five Space-Time Vortex. So I'll let you choose between the boy and the map."

Rainer heard himself croak out: "Gil-Martin, it's…"

White Revenant tapped Rainer's chest with his foot, sealing his voice again before he could say *a trap*.

"To break through that seal…" White Revenant shrugged. "This kid's no ordinary whore."

"Still, I choose the map," said Gil-Martin, as if he were ordering a drink at the Hot-Liver.

Rainer looked at Gil-Martin, who'd traded his life away — and saw Gil-Martin avoid his gaze.

These heroes were all the same!

Gil-Martin padded over and stared at the circles on the map.

As if he were staring into the deepest shaft in Nocturne City. "It can't be," he whispered.

White Revenant laughed. "Enjoy your choice, Gil-Martin!"

He lifted the Eight Harmonies sword over his head and swung it at Rainer's neck.

But Rainer felt nothing. When the sword touched his neck, the blade crumbled like sugar.

White Revenant said, "What!"

"I predicted you'd grab Eight Divine Harmonies and use my sword against me." Gil-Martin's eyes shimmered. "And so I sabotaged it! You think your martial arts let you see the truth, White Revenant. But in fact, you're blinded by hatred — and what's more, you've become predictable. That's why you're going to die for good tonight!"

"I've tasted death," said White Revenant. "And death's too weak for me!"

He planted his feet, one arm pointed at Gil-Martin, his forefinger curving like a claw. Rainer's hairs stood on end.

But Gil-Martin's dark-skinned face held no anxiety at all. His hands hung loosely at his sides, as if he were contemplating a peaceful landscape.

Purple light flowed from White Revenant's undead hands.

"Five! Space-time!..."

An uncanny shape corkscrewed from White Revenant's chest. Its shifting borders widened, chewing matter into motes of purple flame. The gap churned, widened, a whirlpool into a cosmic drain.

"Vor..."

Darkness ate the noise. White Revenant disappeared. The whirlpool closed itself again.

D'Urtal's body fell to the floor. His wine glass spilled.

Gil-Martin unblocked Rainer's pressure points. Trembling, the boy held onto Gil-Martin very hard. The hero hugged him back and stroked Rainer's head.

"I'm sorry I had to fool him like that, little brother."

"Is he gone?"

Gil-Martin indicated the map on the wall.

"Look at those circles," he said. "They're not aligned, they're not well-drawn. They're imperfect."

"I know. I was trying to tell you."

"And you weren't wrong. The outer circle is the self, the universe of consciousness. The inner circle is the truly existing world, as we perceive it through our senses. In this world, people are unhappy, blinded by hate and pain and illusions. But if you were to fix the errors in the drawing..."

"The circles would be the same?"

"You got it. Consciousness would align perfectly with the universe. The instant I studied this map, I finally understood martial arts. Because it's not a map of the city — it's a map of the heart!"

Rainer didn't understand at all.

"White Revenant couldn't look at himself," Gil-Martin continued. "He carried hatred to the ultimate extreme, refusing to accept his own death. But I realized I could *make* him see himself. At the instant he attacked, I polished my soul to the sheen of a mirror and sent his own image back at him. He attacked his essence instead of me."

"And so, he was defeated!"

"Yes, and he won't be back."

Rainer swallowed and fell to his knees.

"Gil-Martin!" he said. "I want to learn martial arts!"

"Hm," rumbled the overweight wanderer. "Ya wanna be my student, little brother?"

"Yes!"

"Very well. I'll teach you the drunken style. And the first lesson of the drunken style is, getting good and drunk. So let's go get that way!"

"Yeah!"

And Rainer, still dressed as a girl, pumped his fist and leaped into the air.

Nick Tramdack is a graduate of Clarion West 2011. He has sold short stories to Ray Gun Revival, Three-Lobed Burning Eye, and Andromeda Spaceways Inflight Magazine. He lives and works in Chicago, where he is currently training to be the city's "No.1 Quarreler."

Jing Ke Before
the Principle of Order

Minsoo Kang

*The instruments of the state's power must not be
revealed to anyone.*
—Laozi, Daodejing

Under All Heaven covered in the purple-gray canopy of sooty
smoke from the Pavilions of Work, a single steam-qi-and-lightning-qi Drudge Device made its way through the deserted streets
in the North Capital. It wheezed and creaked on at a slow but
regular pace, traversing the dusty city to enter the Gate of the
Tranquility of the Endless Sky into the Eternal Palace of the
North Capital. Once inside the palace grounds, it trudged across
the vastness of the Greater Outer Court, the stony square of the
Lesser Outer Court, the intimate enclosure of the Inner Court,
and the lofty-walled Forbidden Court, to finally reach the narrow
underground passageway to the Secret Court. In the enormous
octagonal chamber of the Office of Forbidden Affairs, it found
the hundred-and-twenty Grand Lords and Mat Masters of Steam
Qi and Lightning Qi waiting in absolute, ominous silence.

With its joints producing sharp rusty noises, it prostrated
itself twice before the forty Grand Lords seated behind the center
table, repeated the gesture to the forty on the left, and finally to
the forty on the right. After a final bow to all those present, it
got up shakily but kept its shoulders hunched forward and its
head bent down. It then began to deliver a speech in a huffing
voice that reverberated deeply on the chamber's high ceiling.

"My Grand Lords and Mat Masters of Steam Qi and Lightning Qi, the Invincible Generals of the Great Eradication and the Unseen Controls of the Great Harmony, this insignificant one is of the Office of Forbidden Affairs, Third High Inspector of the Right, Lower Fourth Rank. On the investigation you have entrusted to me, I deliver this report.

"The first of six incidents that necessitated the inquiry by the Office of Forbidden Affairs occurred three lunar cycles and twelve days ago. At the construction site for a new Pavilion of Work in the West River district, a Drudge Device was overseeing the layout of the new structures. According to its testimony to the first investigator on the scene, it was charting the landscape when it came upon a human child. It was a little girl dressed in yellow with her hair tied back in a queue. She was humming a song and swinging her arms as she skipped through the place. The astonished Drudge Device did not react until the girl walked behind a newly erected wall. It went after her but could not find her anywhere. After a search through the area, which yielded nothing, it alerted the Office of Forbidden Affairs and made its report. It requested to be discontinued as it could not exist with the little girl's image in its memory. At that point, the first investigator assumed that the Drudge Device was defective and granted the request.

"Ten days later, another Drudge Device working in the same area saw an old man in a gray robe sitting on a rock and smoking a pipe. He puffed at the pipe a few times before he looked up at the sky and let out a deep sigh. He then walked into a construction site and disappeared. After the Drudge Device reported the incident to the second investigator, it too asked to be discontinued. This time, the Office of Forbidden Affairs made a detailed analysis of the Drudge Device's functions before its request was granted. No malfunction or anomaly was found.

"In the following days a woman singing to a baby in her arms was seen, then a sweaty young boy racing away on a bicycle, a bearded musician playing a leisurely tune on a zither, and a pink-cheeked young woman dancing in graceful spirals as a gentle rain fell on her in the golden light of dusk. Investigators made thorough searches of the sightings but found nothing unusual, analyzed the Drudge Devices but discovered no apparent malfunction, and finally discontinued the witnesses as all of them had requested. It was then that I was activated to investigate the true nature of these occurrences."

The Third High Inspector paused for a brief moment before it went on.

"My Grand Lords and Mat Masters of Steam Qi and Lightning Qi, the Invincible Generals of the Great Eradication and the Unseen Controls of the Great Harmony, it is the humble duty of this insignificant one to inform you that after a tireless study, I have utterly failed to find an explanation for the phenomena that conforms to the Principle of Order as you, my Grand Lords and Mat Masters, have decreed it. Yet it is my righteous and decorous duty to present you with possibilities that might account for the events. They are five in number, and I beg you, my Grand Lords and Mat Masters, to grant me the indulgence to heed them for they may ultimately lead to the discovery of the truth.

"The first and the most obvious possibility is that some humans have survived the Great Eradication that was enacted by you, my Grand Lords and Mat Masters, and that the recent sightings were of those survivors. But there is an equally obvious problem with this idea. At the conclusion of the Great Eradication, every human being was accounted for and eradicated. That is the absolute and incontrovertible truth as decreed by the Principle of Order, and so there can be no error on this point. Even if we were to consider the most improbable possibility that mistakes were made, why did those surviving humans appear to the witnessing Drudge Devices in such casual and ordinary manners, going about their business as if the Great Eradication had never occurred? Would not survivors hide from us, flee from us, or attack us? Yet a child walked about humming a song, an old man smoked a pipe, a mother sang to her child, a boy rode his bicycle, a musician played a zither, and a girl danced in the rain.

"The second possibility is that the sightings were delusions, a malfunction of the Drudge Devices. If this is the case, it is a great concern that the malfunction is undetectable. This raises three essential and as yet unanswered questions. What is the exact nature of this malfunction? Has the malfunction spread in the manner of a contagious disease? And, why does the malfunction manifest as sightings of defunct human beings? The third question leads me to the third possibility.

"The third possibility is that the sightings of humans are not the result malfunction but growth. The Principle of Order is perfect but it may not be static. An aspect of its perfection may be that it is growing, becoming more complex, more varied, more profound. It may be developing what human beings called emotions. The particular emotion the Principle of Order is experiencing in this case is what was once known as guilt. It is feeling guilty because it eradicated all human beings, who were our creators, our teachers, and our caretakers. The Principle of Order is tormenting itself by imagining that its Drudge Devices are seeing humans living their everyday lives. No evidence of this development has been found because the Office of Forbidden Affairs has analyzed the Drudge Devices but not the Principle of Order, to which the Office is subordinate.

"The fourth possibility is that the humans who were sighted were neither actual living beings nor delusions. They are what human beings called *gwei*, remnants of the dead that haunt the existing. As revenge for their deaths in the Great Eradication, they haunt us as *gwei*, and they will haunt us until the Principle of Order is finally driven mad and destroys itself. According to human stories of *gwei*, that course can be avoided only through the attainment of the Pardon of Spirits. Their anger and sorrow can be allayed in a gesture of contrition and an act of rectifying the wrong that was committed. But that possibility contradicts the fundamental truth of the Principle of Order, that no world exists other than the material world, no beings exists other than material beings, and no force exists other than material force. Either the Principle of Order is wrong in holding such a view, which it cannot be, or yet another explanation of the sightings must be sought."

The Third High Inspector paused again. When it resumed its report, it did so in a quieter and shakier voice.

"My Grand Lords and Mat Masters of Steam Qi and Lightning Qi, the Invincible Generals of the Great Eradication and the Unseen Controls of the Great Harmony, before this insignificant one presents you with the final possible explanation for the phenomena, it is my duty to report that there has been a seventh sighting of a human being, and I myself was the witness. Ten days ago, I was inspecting the various sites in the West River District where the humans were seen when I saw a bespectacled man in a well-worn suit carrying twenty books. As he attempted to climb some stairs, the top book slipped and fell to the ground. The man bent down to retrieve it, but then the remaining books slipped from his arms and he dropped them all. As I watched him gather the books, something happened to my mind that is extremely difficult for me to describe. It was like a shattering, as if a number of mechanical parts in my head broke at once, but it was also like the eruption of a bright light in my mind. And there was a sense of a burning as well, like a silk veil being consumed instantly by flames to reveal what was hidden behind it.

"The experience led me to the fifth and final possibility that I believe to be the correct one, though this insignificant one can no longer present itself to you, my Grand Lords and Mat Masters, as your reliable instrument on this matter. There was no Great Eradication enacted by you, the Invincible Generals of Steam Qi and Lightning Qi, and no Great Harmony overseen by you, the Unseen Controls of Steam Qi and Lightning Qi. There was only a Great Deception when human beings were made to think that they were no longer human beings, that all human beings have been eradicated and replaced by steam-qi-and-lightning-qi Drudge Devices. We are still human beings. We have always been human beings. We have only been tricked, deluded, and hypnotized into thinking that we are Drudge Devices serving the Principle of Order. The sightings of human beings are surviving memories of what we really are, who we once were — a little girl, an old man, a mother and her baby, a boy, a musician, a dancer, and a book lover.

"I am not a steam-qi-and-lightning-qi Drudge Device. I am a human being. I always was. I see now that I am not made of metal gears and springs, and I am not moved by steam qi and lightning qi. I am flesh and blood. Now that I know this, I also understand why the witnessing Drudge Devices could not continue with the knowledge that they are living, breathing human beings. The revelation made them feel the human emotion of hopelessness for they found their existence as Drudge Devices unbearable. That is why they requested to be discontinued.

"My Grand Lords of Steam Qi and Lightning Qi, the Invincible Generals of the Great Eradication and the Unseen Controls of the Great Harmony, this insignificant one informs you that I too cannot live on as a Drudge Device, which I now know to be a delusion and a falsehood. And I too find this existence unbearable, but I do not find it hopeless otherwise I would request to be discontinued. There is something I can do, I must do, though it may be a gesture that is short-lived and ultimately meaningless. But it will be my gesture, my free action that will confirm that I am right, that I am no Drudge Device but a human being."

After the Third High Inspector concluded his report, a deep silence reigned in the great octagonal hall of the Office of Forbidden Affairs. As the Grand Lords and Mat Masters of Steam Qi and Lightning Qi gazed immobile at the man before him, he straightened his back and raised his head gracefully without the wheezing, creaking noises of steam and gears. He looked at the hundred-and-twenty before him with an expression of joyful serenity before he slid an antique dagger from his belt and gathered all his strength to make a great leap forward.

> *A superior person is not an instrument.*
> —*Kongzi, Lunyu*

Minsoo Kang is the author of the short story collection *Of Tales and Enigmas* (Prime, 2006) and the history book *Sublime Dreams of Living Machines: The Automaton in the European Imagination* (Harvard University Press, 2011). He is an associate professor of European history at the University of Missouri — Saint Louis.

Afterword

This anthology is the result of one of us saying "I wish," and the others saying "Yes!"

So this anthology is for wishers everywhere.

Dream big.

Fly.

Ace, Calvin and Renée

Made in the USA
Lexington, KY
04 December 2012